CODY ROSE

FC HENDERSON

The contents of this book come solely from the author's imagination. With the exception of a few publicly known figures any resemblance to actual persons is strictly coincidental.

Copyright December, 2016   all rights reserved

ISBN 10 – 1540810720

OTHER WORKS BY FC HENDERSON

- EARLY RETIREMENT (Murder in Daytona)
- SISTERHOOD OF THE SKULL & ROSES
- AN AMERICAN IDOL (The Illuminati Conspiracy)
- UNEXPLAINABLE THINGS (a collection of short stories)

All books available for purchase on Amazon or by contacting the author directly at
FCH32174@YAHOO.COM

This book is dedicated to the millions of people who suffer from life threatening illnesses every year In this country. And the countless dedicated professionals who care for them.

CODY ROSE
CHAPTER ONE

When the senior psychotherapist at Saint Raphael's Hospital appeared in Cody Rose's doorway to introduce himself he was roundly ignored. His new patient's attention was fixated on an obscure painting hanging on the wall across from her hospital bed. The artwork appeared to be one of those inexpensive prints you can purchase in the homewares section of most department stores. It might set you back thirty bucks or so, if you were so inclined.

After several unsuccessful attempts to get Cody's attention the therapist decided to place himself between his patient and the object of her contemplation. Had he properly anticipated Cody's fascination with the painting Ted probably would have let her be, but that wasn't the case. He too was fixated on something at that moment. Namely completing his morning rounds. In addition to Cody, psychotherapist Ted Grace had half a dozen other patients to get to before noon.

The painting that Cody was obsessing over appeared to be religious in nature. It depicted a thick wooden door encased in an old stone wall. Floating just above the door were two chubby cherubim, their wings spread as if protecting the entrance from outside influence. As far as Ted was concerned the mundane piece was completely forgettable. In fact he'd been in that hospital room hundreds of times over the years and never even noticed it until now.

His patient on the other hand studied the painting as if it were Leonardo Da Vinci's *'Mona Lisa'*. The dying woman's dogged determination to disengage herself from outside distractions was obvious. If her therapist had not positioned himself at the foot of her bed she would have lay there staring at that painting until she took her last breath. Ted might have felt a certain degree of guilt for interrupting her if it were not for the fact doing so provided him the opportunity he needed to reach her.

The fifty-three year old woman had been rushed to Saint Raphael's several days before after suffering a seizure. Medical tests confirmed she was in renal failure. Cody Rose's kidneys had stopped functioning.

It wasn't long before her doctors discovered there was something even more sinister than renal failure going on with this patient. Her failing kidneys were but a symptom. Cody had a much deeper problem. She was suffering from a rare medical disorder known as Lesch-Nyhan Syndrome.

The diagnosis completely eliminated any chance of Cody being considered for a kidney transplant. Her body would only attack a new kidney, rendering it worthless too. The situation was dire. The woman was in the final stages of a life threatening illness for which there was no cure. She would not be leaving Saint Raphael's Hospital. At least not alive.

Lesch-Nyhan Syndrome can be downright intolerable. It is not uncommon to learn someone suffering from the disorder has taken their own life. Ted could only imagine the anger his new patient must be feeling. Woe to be cursed with such an affliction. The fact Cody hadn't uttered a word to anyone since arriving at the hospital was completely understandable.

It was the psychotherapist hope and desire to bring the dying woman some sense of peace and comfort in her final days. After all it was his responsibility. As the hospital's senior palliative care specialist he had developed the program Saint Raphael's was using to treat its terminal patients.

"Tis a perfectly lovely morning, is it not, Ms. Rose" Ted had cheerfully stated upon his arrival to her room that first time. *"Allow me to introduce myself. My name is Ted Grace. I am going to be your therapist. So how are we feeling today?"*

When Ted got no response to his idiomatic pronouncement he repeated it, this time with even more gusto. He knew Cody could hear him. Nothing in her medical file indicated there was any type of hearing loss. The therapist knew his battle was going to be breaching the emotional barrier Cody had wrapped herself in. It was a commonly used defense mechanism. Facing certain death people often shut themselves off from the outside world.

By interrupting Cody's concentration the psychotherapist hoped to cross over that boundary.

He spent a considerable amount of time with Cody over the next few days. Eventually she came out of her shell. What Ted discovered was a woman of thought and thoughtfulness. Cody refused to let the hand she'd been dealt dictate how she would spend the time she had been given.

She hadn't shut the world out because she was angry. Nor was it because she was fearful of what lie ahead. The reason Cody closed herself off from the outside world was because she didn't want others to be negatively impacted by her suffering. She was willing to forfeit her own solace for their sake. It was an act of love.

Often times Ted would stop in for a visit after his shift had ended. He was a bachelor. There was no place he needed to be that wouldn't be there when he was ready to leave. The therapist would sit and listen for hours as Cody reflected on various chapters of her life. She never held anything back. There was no guilt or shame. It was as if the dying woman needed to confess her sins to someone before it was too late.

During these visits Cody would often refer to the painting on her wall. She'd ask Ted, *"Is that not the most beautiful work of art you have ever seen? Is it not a true masterpiece?"*

In all honesty it wasn't. Ted thought the painting was rather bland. It was something he might put up on the wall as an afterthought, and in a not very conspicuous place. The piece wasn't even signed. That was a telltale sign right there. Any artist worth his weight would sign his own work. *"In all honesty I've not much of an eye for art,"* Ted would unpretentiously reply before adding, *"They say beauty is in the eye of the beholder, Ms. Rose."*

It didn't take long before the psychotherapist realized Cody never displayed any sign of discomfort whenever she was talking about the painting. He knew the medication she was on would provide her some relief, but still her pain had to be significant. One day Ted worked up the nerve to ask her about it. That's when he discovered Cody was a woman of faith.

Cody claimed God was communicating comfort and healing to her through the painting on her wall. She was certain Jesus was on the other side of that thick wooden door waiting to greet her into His kingdom.

The idea of religion was lost on a man who looked into the eyes of death on a daily basis. Ted had attended church as a child, but those days were long gone. He listened to Cody's banter, but the psychotherapist secretly questioned what kind of God would allow one of his children to suffer in this way.

It didn't really matter what he believed anyway. It's what Cody believed that was important. If the terminally ill woman's faith in an invisible sovereign would help her complete her journey then so be it.

Ted had to admit he was impressed by Cody's obsession with the painting on her wall. She saw things in it he simply missed. Like the plethora of color in the stone surrounding the door. She pointed out the hints of magenta and deep purple that could be made out in the crevices between the stone. They were bluish red, like the meat of a plum. One had to look really close to notice.

There were other things too. Where he saw an old weathered door Cody saw streaks of amber and cinnamon hidden in the fractal lines of the wood. The two cherubim hovering above the entrance were a muted pink. Ted thought they appeared powdery, like sugar angels that might crumble and fall at any moment. Cody was quick to point out the undeniable masculinity of the two cherubim. The thickness of their meaty bodies and the muscles in their calves. The more she spoke the more the therapist began to appreciate the piece. Still, it was just an obscure painting.

Ted truly hoped Cody would see that he was there for her. He had tried to interject what his job was into their conversation. How the intervention program he had developed could help her cope with her situation. For all the good it did the therapist may as well have been talking to a brick wall. The conversation always made its way back to that damn painting. Cody Rose's door to nowhere.

The following Saturday morning Ted was home making himself some breakfast when he felt the sudden urge to get dressed and drive over to the hospital. He didn't know why. It was supposed to be his day off. It was as if some invisible force was willing his steps. He had no sense of impending doom. The thought of Cody dying in the night never crossed his mind. In fact Ted stopped at a florist shop along the way to pick up a dozen roses for Cody's nightstand.

The poor woman hadn't received a single get well card since she arrived at Saint Raphael's. Not one. She'd had not one visitor either. You would have thought someone who lived the life she did would be deluged with well-wishers, but that wasn't the case. Ted was it. He would be the one chosen to witness her departure when that time came. And it would be his honor. But perhaps I'm getting ahead of myself. Best we start at the beginning...

CODY ROSE
CHAPTER TWO

From the moment she was born Cody was the apple of her father's eye. Six pounds and twelve ounces, with flaming red hair and brilliant blue eyes. God help the poor bastard who broke her heart. Tony Rose told that to everyone he came into contact with in the weeks following the birth of his baby daughter.

Tony was not a big man, but he was tough. Tough as the iron spikes Delaware Tioga paid him and his crew to drive through the wooden railroad ties the company was laying between the cities of Binghamton and Elmira, New York.

The regional railroad had recently 'merged' with Erie Rail, a small local line. Tony and his crew were laying new track to tie the two lines together. Delaware executives intended to capture the burgeoning commercial coal market opening up throughout western Pennsylvania.

When discussing this particular topic it would be wise to use the word 'merged' with tongue in cheek. The truth is Delaware Tioga pulled off a hostile takeover that would prove impossible in the business world of today. So hostile was it the governor of New York had to intervene.

Delaware Tioga employed a small army of mercenaries intent on driving Erie Rail out of business. The hired thugs were ordered to derail the smaller company's rail cars by flipping switches along the track. Erie Rail responded by hiring mercenaries of their own to protect their property.

The entire ordeal came to a head in a railroad tunnel outside the village of Painted Post, New York. That's where the two adversaries conjoined. The hired thugs attacked each other with all manner of weapons, forcing the governor to call in the state militia to end the conflict.

Realizing they couldn't muscle their competition out of business Delaware Tioga executives decided to take the path of least resistance. They encouraged all their major shareholders to purchase stock in the smaller railroad. When a sufficient number of shares had switched hands Delaware executives would call for a special election. The two companies would then 'merge' to form one large line.

Upon learning of the planned coup attorneys for Erie Rail filed a lawsuit against their larger competitor insisting the forced merger be thwarted. You would think New York State's Supreme Court would have realized what was going on and stopped Delaware Tioga in its tracks. You would be wrong.

Delaware Tioga Railroad was a very powerful company with very powerful men at the helm. Men who got where they were by playing hardball. The court found Erie Rail's case to be without merit. The decision was handed down one day after the chief justice of the court received a generous contribution from an anonymous donor. It was with this newly 'merged' company Tony Rose found employment.

The country was expanding and rail was the preferred mode of transportation used by nearly every business with something to sell. Men with brawn were in high demand, especially if they had thick skin and a workman's ethic to go along with it. A few months after signing on as a laborer Tony Rose was given his own crew and tasked with laying sixty miles of new track. They were given thirty days to complete the assignment. If the men were successful they would continue to be employed by the Delaware Tioga Railroad. If not, well...there was always the Pennsylvania coal mines.

Needless to say they were successful. A few of the men found they couldn't pull their weight under Tony's tutelage but those that stayed came to love and respect him. Tony Rose was not one to let the other guy do what he himself would not. If a job needed doing he was right there working side by side with his men getting it done. And if someone on his crew had a need Tony didn't hesitate going to bat for them.

There was this one Irish spike driver who received word his father had been killed during a barroom brawl back in the old country. The young bloke's mother and three sisters were left destitute. America was beckoning but financially it was impossible for them to make the journey. Tony went to his boss on the crewman's behalf. Next thing he knew arrangements were made to bring the young Irishman's family over to America all expenses paid.

As for Tony, he was just happy to have a job. He rarely asked for anything for himself. Tony appreciated the fact his employer had entrusted him with his own crew. He would never do anything to jeopardize that. There did come a time when he did have to ask a favor though. It was three years after Cody was born.

The last thing a father needs to hear is that his little girl is sick. Especially when the economy has tanked and the nation is about to entire what would become known as *'The Great Depression.'* At the age of three Cody was diagnosed with cerebral palsy.

She had been dealing with an acute loss of motor skills for several months. Cody suffered painful muscle spasms and went through debilitating fits. Doctors were baffled by her symptoms at first. After conducting multiple rounds of tests they confirmed their diagnosis.

Time would prove those doctors wrong. What Cody actually had was a rare medical disorder called Lesch-Nyhan Syndrome. The doctors couldn't be faulted for their misdiagnosis however. Lesch-Nyhan had yet to be identified. That wouldn't happen for another forty years.

LNS is a rare disorder to be sure. Made rarer still by the fact it is almost exclusively a males only illness. Girls do not get what Cody got. Less than one in three million… according to the odds. Sometimes fate can deal a losing hand.

When Tony told his employers about Cody's diagnosis they stood by him. He was transferred to a job riding the very rails he and his crew had laid. First as a fireman stoking the boilers of the steam locomotives, then later when the railroad switched to diesel power as an office foreman scheduling the maintenance crews. The move allowed him to be home more nights than not. His little girl needed him, and Tony Rose had always been a man people could count on.

CODY ROSE
CHAPTER THREE

Over the next few years Cody's symptoms dissipated somewhat. Her father took credit for that, telling everyone who would listen his daughter's condition improved because he was around more. She did suffer occasional muscle spasms, and her joints would ache from gout, but the attacks became more and more sporadic.

One unpleasant side effect Cody had to deal with was something doctors termed *Precocious Puberty.* By the age of ten Cody had physically develop years ahead of other girls her age. She grew pubic hair, and her voice lowered an octave or two. Her breasts and genitals took on a much more feminine tone. By age twelve Cody Rose was for all intents a woman. Like many young women her hormones raged.

One of the saddest things about a situation like that is that a preadolescent mind does not keep up with the physical changes taking place in a pubescent body. As a fifth grader Cody Rose was taken advantage of by one of her male teachers.

Dean Russell had been keeping tabs on his overdeveloped student ever since she entered his classroom. The thirty two year old father of three had spent the entire school year fantasizing about Cody. At first he thought she must have been kept back a year or two. How else does a girl like that end up in fifth grade?

Though he fought the urge to act on his immoral inclinations the teacher found he just couldn't resist the temptation. His sex life at home had become hum drum. After bearing him three children Russell's wife showed no interest in producing any more offspring. When the opportunity presented itself the educator jumped.

Russell approached it innocently enough. If anyone were to question his motives the teacher would be able to quash their concerns without further inquiry. He had been tasked with directing the school's Christmas play that year. A chore Russell volunteered for at the beginning of the school year. His reasons were personal. The play would provide him a respite from the boredom that was his home life. It wasn't until that moment he thought to involve his overly developed student in the production.

Besides teaching fifth grade and directing the Christmas play Dean Russell pulled lunch monitor duty two days a week. Tuesdays and Fridays would find him in the cafeteria seeking an unobstructed view of Cody Rose. He would lean his back against the wall and let his imagination run wild.

One day Cody lingered at the table while her classmates rushed out of the cafeteria at the sound of the bell. Russell watched from his perch as the other lunch monitors joined the students in the mass exodus. When the coast was clear the teacher approached the object of his attention.

"How's it going Cody" Russell asked his prey, a dubious smile on his face. Dean was not a big guy. He stood five foot, seven inches. A mere inch taller than his student. With no facial hair he looked young for his age.

The curvaceous twelve year old had remained in the cafeteria to finish up an English project that was due. She looked up from her paper and answered, *"I'm doing great, Mr. Russell. How are you?"*

Cody truly was as innocent as the freshly fallen snow. An inculpable child living in an adult size body. Russell didn't care. He pounced. *"I'm glad you asked, Cody. I don't know if you heard but I am directing the Christmas play this year. I can't seem to find a student mature enough to play the lead role. You don't happen to act, do you?"*

The line was cast. Now to reel in the catch...

"Me," Cody replied, a look of astonishment on her face. *"You want me to be in your play, Mr. Russell? No, I couldn't!"*

"Why not," the nefarious teacher responded. *"I think you would be a natural. You must know you are the prettiest girl in school. You would be perfect for the role."*

Russell could see the wheels turning in the child's brain. He jiggled the line hoping she'd bite. *"You should see the gowns the lead actress will be wearing. You would look beautiful in them, Cody Rose."* The depraved orator paused to consider his next comments carefully, than delivered. *"With a body like yours men will be lining up to ask you out. I know I'm your teacher Cody, but... My God you are an attractive young woman..."*

Cody felt her face flush. She was well aware of the fact most men looked at her differently than they did other girls her age. It made her very self-conscious.

But it was also quite flattering. The hormones that had been bubbling up inside Cody's quickly changing body spilled over like a shaken soda bottle. A grown man had just complimented her. The look he gave her had not gone unnoticed. Other men had given her that same look before. Cody always felt awkward when a man looked at her like that. Especially when the man was her father.

Yes... Her father. Tony couldn't help noticing his daughter's rapid rise to womanhood. His little girl had leap frogged over several stages of childhood development. She went from being this chubby little moppet with two missing front teeth to a buxom young woman that men craved. He hated it!

"You really think I'm pretty" Cody responded, her face pink as a rose petal. It seemed different this time. She didn't understand why, but she couldn't deny the wetness she felt down below. Most twelve year old girls would have thought what Mr. Russell said was gross. Most preteen girls wouldn't like being come on to by a grown man. It would make them very uncomfortable. Her response surprised her. It came from that place inside. That bubbling caldron.

"I find you very attractive," the conniving teacher continued. *"You are different than the other schoolgirls, Cody. You must know that..."*

She was stimulated to be sure. Cody had never been talked to like that before. Not by anyone. Heck she'd never even had a boyfriend before. The twelve year old's hormones beckoned her to think forbidden thoughts foreign to a preadolescent mind.

Now that the ball was rolling Dean Russell didn't want to stop. Unfortunately the second lunch bell rang informing those who had lingered they were now late for class. *"Shit... We have to go,"* the teacher announced. *"I wish all my students were as mature as you, Cody Rose."*

The two rushed out of the lunch room together. Russell checked the hall to see if anyone was around, then he turned to face his prey. *"Cody, I want you to stop by the auditorium after school. I need to show you those gowns. You can even try them on if you like. I want to see you in those dresses, Cody... Very much. Think about it, okay?"*

With that Russell nodded for his student to get going. He watched as she disappeared around the corner. Visions of those preadolescent bouncing breasts remained implanted in his brain the remainder of the day.

✝

CODY ROSE
CHAPTER FOUR

Cody's father became more ambivalent towards his daughter with each passing day. His little girl had become something he couldn't deal with. She had grown up before her time. How does a father take a vivacious fully developed preteen like Cody and sit her on his knee? How does he take her by the hand and walk her around his neighborhood? He knew people would talk. They would point, and stare, and whisper.

What he couldn't seem to understand was that his little girl didn't grow up before her time. Inside Cody was still Cody. A twelve year old girl with a utopian view of the world. All the unsolicited attention she garnered because of her looks was brought on by a medical condition she had no control over.

Tony was focusing on the precocious puberty part of his daughter's medical condition while forgetting about the other symptoms. Symptoms so severe they caused Cody's joints to swell to the point she could not bend her fingers or make a fist. So severe she sometimes wasn't able to wear shoes.

Pain would shoot through Cody's back and down her legs like she had been shot. There was no escape. All the poor child could do was grin and bear it. Then almost overnight her body changes and suddenly people are looking at her like she is a freak.

If the symptoms Cody experienced during her childhood had not diminished she may have become one of those Lesch-Nyhan sufferers who uncontrollably turn on themselves. There are case studies of people with LNS who self-mutilate, or worse...commit suicide.

It is a horrendous illness to be sure. If the worst thing Cody did was react impulsively to the immoral advances of a corrupt teacher, well who are we to judge?

Tony Rose could not, would not, accept his daughter's predicament. At a time when she needed him the most Tony chose to withhold his affection for her. He wished he'd stayed in his old job laying rail. At least back then Tony could pretend his life was normal. His little girl would have remained just that. At least inside his head.

He had started drinking shortly after Cody was first diagnosed with her illness. He didn't realize it, but alcohol consumption was his way of coping with the stress. Watching your children suffer and not being able to help can wear on a man. Tony's drinking was an act of desperation, done to compensate for the lack of control he felt over the situation. Over the years it just got worse.

Tony Rose wasn't a homebound drunk. He did his drinking at the bar. The idea was to escape reality, not inebriate in the midst of it. Shortly after prohibition ended saloons began popping up on every Main Street in America. Many a man took to downing a shot and a beer at the local tavern, despite the fact the country was still in the midst of the great depression. It was at one of these drinking establishments Tony met the woman who would rescue him from his fate.

He wasn't looking to leave his family for someone else. It just sort of happened. Margaret Mayweather was a forty-two year old divorcee with a strong appetite for blue collar working men. Especially men with big muscles. What she didn't have an appetite for was sickly children.

As fate would have it the day Tony chose to leave happened to be the same day Cody's teacher preyed on her. Coincidence can be cruel. She would learn her father had abandoned her less than thirty minutes after succumbing to her teacher's despicable immoral advances.

The twelve year old was clueless. It is altogether fortunate her molester shied away from vaginal penetration. Dean Russell was smart enough to know leaving a seminal fluid trail could be disastrous. He settled for some heavy fondling.

When she entered the auditorium that afternoon Russell was hiding in the shadows, concealed by a dark velveteen stage curtain. The corrupt teacher was invisible to anyone viewing from the front. He watched in pathogenic anticipation as Cody pranced down the middle aisle. The child's gait had a measured movement that told him he was not going to have to work very hard to get what he wanted... Not today.

"Psssst... Cody... I'm over here," Russell whispered after reassuring himself they were alone. *"Behind the curtain."*

The only illumination came from a single forty watt light bulb dangling from a wire near the rear exit. Russell had killed the rest of the lights at the fuse box while awaiting his victim's arrival.

Doing so was a conscious act. The educator knew full well what he was about to do. He was preparing to subject this innocent twelve year old neophyte to a shameful act. He was going to take advantage of a subservient child. One who was immature far beyond what her physical appearance might suggest.

"The evil that men do long outlives them." That particular Shakespearean quote was in this case dead on. Cody arrived at the rear of the stage to find her teacher waiting there, his manhood fully exposed.

According to New York State Penal Law a child Cody's age is incapable of giving her consent to what happened next. Dean Russell took the twelve year old's hand and placed it someplace it had absolutely no business being. Shaking with excitement the unprincipled teacher camouflaged the act by placing his own hand on top of his student's. Then he leaned forward and kissed Cody on the mouth.

Encouraged by Cody's failure to resist the nefarious teacher coaxed the child to her knees and gave her one final instruction. At twelve years of age what Cody really needed was the firm hand of a loving parent to guide her through this difficult stage of life. Unfortunately that wasn't going to happen. Her daddy was already gone...

New York State Penal Code
Title H   Article: 130   Sexual Offenses

Section 130.05 - Lack of consent:

Subsection 3.
A person is deemed incapable of giving consent when he or she is less than seventeen years old.

Section 130.50

Criminal sexual act in the first degree. A person age eighteen and above is guilty of a criminal sexual act in the first degree when he or she engages in sexual conduct with another person and;

Subsection 4.

That person is under age thirteen.

Criminal sexual act in the first degree is a class B felony. It is punishable by up to twenty-five years to life imprisonment.

....

As illustrated in the aforementioned New York State Penal Code a twelve year old child is considered incapable of giving her consent to what Cody's teacher had her do.

†

CODY ROSE
CHAPTER FIVE

Cody didn't know how she was going to face her father when she got home. He was sure to know. What she had done was written all over her face. She was convinced of that.

Mr. Russell had made her promise not to tell anyone. *"NOT A SOUL,"* he'd demanded. The teacher was adamant about it. If he were to lose his job there were no others. The country was in the midst of The Great Depression. Families had lost everything they owned. Joblessness was tantamount to homelessness. Dean Russell and his family would be on the street.

Cody didn't really understand the economic consequences her teacher would face if it were discovered what he'd done, never mind the legal ramifications. She figured Mr. Russell was afraid his wife would find out and divorce him. Her silence was his only saving grace.

Dean Russell avoided her after that. Cody never did get to act in the Christmas play. She never even got to try on those gowns her teacher had told her about. Cody figured she must have done something wrong. Perhaps she wasn't experienced enough for him. She would keep her vow of silence though. Nobody would understand anyway.

Discovering her father had left her mother for another woman took the wind out of Cody's sails. Her carnal desires continued to permeate her thoughts but she didn't act on them again. Not for a long while... Then she met someone.

The guy's name was Dan White. He was a twenty-two year old rookie police officer from a neighboring town. At twenty-two years of age Dan was seven years older than Cody. Though a lot closer in age than her teacher had been the guy was still too old to be having a relationship with a fifteen year old. She was jail bait and Dan White knew it. That didn't stop him.

Cody's mother encouraged her to date the young man despite the age difference. He had earned favored status in the area after being featured in the local news for rescuing a child who'd fallen through the ice. The girl had been walking on the frozen pond when it gave way. His quick actions almost certainly saved her life. Besides, he was from a good family. For some reason that seemed to carry a lot of weight with Cody's mom.

It is by the grace of God Cody didn't get pregnant. Researchers have since learned her illness is hereditary. Lesch-Nyhan is passed on almost exclusively to a woman's male offspring. It has something to do with the fact men only have one X chromosome. The mutation, caused by an inherited defective gene, has to come from a person with two X chromosomes. In other words, a female. Any male child born of Cody would be predestined to carry the syndrome.

She dated Dan White for a little over a year. The two young lovers broke up after Cody's symptoms came rushing back with a vengeance one summer day. They were out on the front porch having iced tea when all of a sudden Cody started flailing her arms wildly about in an uncontrollable fit. Dan watched in horror as his girlfriend hysterically pummeled herself black and blue.

When the strange behavior subsided Dan tried to help Cody out of her chair. The minute her feet hit the floor Cody's legs went limp as jelly. She would spend the next two years confined to a wheelchair.

Dan White just up and disappeared. The last thing the young police officer needed was a paraplegic for a girlfriend. Cody would eventually discover his whereabouts, but not until years later.

In the meantime her father and his mistress cleaned up their act. They bought a house in Binghamton and settled down. Tony Rose took an administrative post with the railroad. Something he swore he would never do. He spent his days calculating labor cost while Margaret got involved with the local church. His new wife was a Baptist by birth. She and Tony eventually became deacons of the congregation. Go figure!

As she got older Cody had long periods of respite from her affliction. During those times one would be hard pressed to identify her as being handicapped. Other than a slight gimp in her gait and an occasional contraction in her muscles no one could tell. By age twenty Cody was back in the saddle so to speak.

Roles for women were rapidly changing. The world was now at war. Many women Cody's age went to work in munitions factories or became skilled in the construction trades. She went to college.

Universities needed to fill the gap left by all the young men going off to war. Many were more than eager to enroll women.

Ithaca College offered Cody a full scholarship to help pave the way. The campus was only thirty miles from her house.

Cody's mom was now working for Ma Bell as an inward line operator. She handled incoming calls sent from the company's main switchboard in Buffalo. Her job put her in touch with just about every person in town.

On occasion Mrs. Rose would listen in on people's private conversations. She would never divulge anyone's secrets, but Cody's mom learned a whole lot of stuff about her neighbors. It opened her eyes to things she never dreamed possible. Things like the shenanigans going on down at the local church, or the way some of the town's upper crust really felt about each other.

Cody loved her mother dearly. She often referred to her with terms of endearment, using words like *Honey* and *Sweetie* and *Beloved.* One would assume it was because of how her mother handled her daughter's affliction so selflessly. Mrs. Rose was devoted to seeing that her child live a full and happy life.

When the day came for Cody to leave for college a neighbor let her borrow his truck to move her things. The pickup had a hole in the exhaust pipe so big Cody's cat could have crawled inside and had kittens. You could hear that old truck coming from a mile away.

Yes, Cody had a cat. An orange polydactyl as it were. She hadn't planned on taking the big footed fur ball with her but the darn thing jumped in the cab of the truck before Cody had a chance to close the door. When she climbed up on Cody's shoulders it was a done deal. The two of them drove the entire way to Ithaca like that.

Cody dated a young man named Herman Peel that first year in college. Herman was an upperclassman two years ahead of her. He would one day become a very successful writer. His most famous work is a novel called THE DANCE OF THE SAINTS, which won the Pulitzer Prize for Literature in 1955. Their relationship didn't last very long. Surprisingly it was Cody who broke it off. She met someone else.

At the beginning of her junior year Cody moved into an off campus apartment. She shared a house with four other girls, all of whom were seniors. One of her housemates would become Cody's lover. A young woman named Torrie Leeter.

The two only knew each other casually at first. The only time they ever spoke was when passing each other in the hallway. Even then it was just a quick hello.

At first Cody didn't pick up on the fact her roommates were all lesbians. Most people would have come to that conclusion pretty quick. Not Cody. At the age of twenty-three she was still quite naïve.

The overprotected girl had never known anyone who was gay. At least no one that admitted to it. Homosexuality was not only a sin... In the 1940s it was against the law. Obviously there were gay people back then, but society snubbed their noses at them. They were morally corrupt. Their spiritual flags flew at half-mast. Anyone even remotely considered as queer would be castigated.

Cody's eyes were finally opened when the landlady invited her tenants to a house party she was hosting. The woman was a physical education instructor at Cornell, the Ivy League school on the opposite side of town. She also coached the women's swim team. Wishing to maintain some semblance of separation from the school that employed her the landlady would only rent her apartment to students from Ithaca College.

When Cody arrived at the party she was amazed to find it a gender specific event. Her landlady greeted her at the door, then introduced her to a woman she identified as *"My partner."* Her name was Eve.

After she finished exchanging pleasantries Cody made her way to the makeshift bar set up on the far side of the living room. Torrie Leeter was standing there mixing herself a drink when Cody got showed up and the two housemates struck up a conversation.

Sensing Cody was a bit confused about the single sex makeup of the guests Torrie tried to explain what was going on. It took a moment for Cody to process the information, but once she understood she was okay with it. *"To each her own I guess,"* is how she responded.

At first Cody was quite surprised to learn her landlady and housemates were all lesbians, but once she put the pieces together the puzzle seemed to fit.

Torrie Leeter was a pretty girl, but the way she carried herself belied the fact. There was a toughness to her. Something about her told the fellas, *"Don't bother… I'm not interested."*

Torrie was far from being the most androgynous of Cody's housemates. That distinction went to a girl named Jamie. Jamie always dressed in slacks and men's shirts, and she never wore make-up. That's not all. Jamie was a jack of all trades. When it came to making repairs around the house everyone knew who to turn to. I guess you could say Jamie was your stereotypical gay girl.

Cody discovered her other two housemates were a couple. The two girls were inseparable. Denise Carter and Jill Johnson arrived at the house party shortly after Cody did. They taught their naïve housemate how to dance the jitterbug that night. Later in the evening Torrie Leeter would show Cody a few more dance steps, this time between the sheets. It turned out to be one of those life altering moments.

✝

CODY ROSE
CHAPTER SIX

As the decade came to a close Cody learned about the plight of her former police officer boyfriend. After witnessing Cody's frightening episode on her mother's front porch that day he decided not to stick around. He went and enlisted in the army.

Who could fault him? Most men would have run. The young police officer was a happy, healthy, carefree guy in the prime of his life. Why would he want to be stuck with a sick girlfriend whose affliction caused her to attack her own body for no apparent reason? It made no sense.

He left for basic training three months to the day after the Japanese bombed Pearl Harbor. March 7th, 1942. Following basic training Dan was assigned to the 502nd Parachute Infantry Battalion headquartered in Fort Bragg, South Carolina.

His placement with the 502nd was no accident. It was due to the fact he'd been a decorated police officer in civilian life. The entire battalion was made up of what the army considered to be top of the line recruits.

That fact caused problems later that summer when the 502nd was integrated into the 101st Airborne Division. Reason being the 101st was mostly made up of less desirable, less experienced draftees.

Many of the division's soldiers were not yet jump qualified. Over the next six months the entire 101st took part in some of the most grueling war games ever conducted by the armed forces. The intent was to prepare every single soldier for what lie ahead. The invasion of Europe...

The 101st Airborne lead America's armed forces into battle on the beaches of Normandy, but their mission began long before the actual invasion took place. Nine months before to be exact. That's when they boarded naval transport vessels and were shipped across the Atlantic.

Dan White's battalion arrived in England on October 18, 1943. Known as the *'Five-O-Deuce,'* the sixteen hundred men who made up the battalion came prepared to continue their trek across the English Channel and do battle with Hitler and his Nazi minions. Instead the men discovered their training was to continue. They spent the next seven months taking twenty-five mile hikes across the English countryside and engaging in close combat exercises.

An ironic twist to the United States Army's war time training strategy happened just before the actual invasion was to take place. The Five-O-Deuce was selected to take part in a drop training exercise along England's western coast. High winds and rough landings resulted in over four hundred injuries that day. Most of the injured soldiers were unable to take part in the actual invasion when it took place three weeks later.

Dan White was part of the initial wave of paratroopers to depart for the French coast. His platoon's mission was to secure the causeways leading inland from Utah Beach. That meant destroying a battery of German artillery set up outside the French village of Ste Martin-de-Varreville.

So many things went wrong during the D-Day invasion it is amazing the allied forces were eventually successful. There was heavy cloud cover that night. When army transport planes broke through the clouds they were met with fierce anti-aircraft fire. Many of them were shot down before they had a chance to deliver their human loads.

More than a few of the transport planes were being flown by inexperienced pilots. Some of them were unable to distinguish the blackness of the land from the churning dark waters of the English Channel. A few dropped their cargo before ever reaching shore. Consequently many paratroopers drowned.

Dan's platoon made it through. Unfortunately they landed five miles east of their intended drop zone. It was simple blind luck that the former police officer survived the drop at all. Nearly half the men who jumped were cut down by enemy gun fire before they ever hit the ground. Dan's platoon leader was one of the casualties.

A corporal named Chas Albright took command. As officer-in-charge he ordered the nine remaining members of the platoon to abandon their radios and turn off their beacons. They were so far from their intended drop zone Corporal Albright didn't want others from the regiment getting killed or captured trying to find them.

Knowing that regular army troops would be landing on the beaches by morning light the depleted platoon made their way back towards the coast. Corporal Albright's plan was simple. Disrupt the Germans in whatever capacity his men could muster.

He hoped to run into others from the Five-0-Deuce, but that didn't happen. His platoon was captured.

It happened almost by accident. A troop of German MP's were on patrol in the countryside seeking out French resistance fighters. The Germans knew the small but determined resistance would be aiding allied pilots when the much anticipated invasion finally came.

The MP's, officially known as the Feldjaeger, had orders to shoot anyone suspected of being part of the resistance. They were also to keep an eye out for any German soldiers trying to avoid the coming invasion. Deserters were to be shot on the spot.

Dan's platoon was following a line of hedges up a hill when one of them tripped causing his rifle to discharge. As luck would have it the Feldjaeger were fifty paces behind them following the same hedge line. It was so dark out that night the two groups could have passed within a few feet of each other without realizing the other was there, had the American soldier not dropped his rifle.

The sound of the discharge took the Feldjaeger by surprise. They dove for cover. Not realizing the German MP's were nearby the paratrooper whose gun had inadvertently gone off started cussing. His lack of judgment told the enemy right where the American paratroopers were.

A firestorm of bullets followed as the Feldjaeger opened up with automatic rifles. Eventually the platoon was surrounded.

Four of Dan's comrades were killed in the onslaught. One of them being Corporal Chas Albright.

The remaining paratroopers were transported to a Nazi base camp about a mile away. They spent the remainder of the night being interrogated by German army officers. In the morning they were placed on a rail car and transported to a Dulag deep inside Germany.

 The Dulags were run by the German SS. If an enemy soldier had any useful information this is where the Nazi's would extract it from them. If a soldier somehow survived the interrogation, and most didn't, they were assigned to a work camp. Dan was sent to Stalag III.

Stalag III was located some thirty miles from Berlin. Though the camp could house over forty thousand prisoners of war at full capacity only eight thousand were kept there at any one time. The remaining prisoners were forced to work in various munitions factories located throughout the area. The rules of the Geneva Convention permitted POW work camps during World War II but they expressly forbade combatants from forcing those captured to manufacture war materials.

The Nazis weren't too concerned about following that particular rule. Records found after the war show Dan White was assigned to a weapons manufacturing plant located in the city of Brandenburg. The entire plant was reduced to rubble during an air raid conducted by the Soviet Red Air Force on Christmas Day, 1944.

When Russian soldiers arrived in Brandenburg several months later they discovered the Nazis had lined up any POW's who survived the raid and summarily cut them down. Dan White was one of the first to be murdered.

Information about Hitler's forced labor program is available to the public through the German government's national archives. The Nazis did an amazing job of record keeping. They kept volumes of data on the many thousands of prisoners they enslaved during the war.

The information includes the names and serial numbers of every POW taken into custody. Dan White's records were there, as were his army issued dog tags and his Screaming Eagles paratrooper patch. Also in his file was a photograph. Anyone who knew her would recognize the young woman in the photo. It was Cody Rose.

✝

CODY ROSE
CHAPTER SEVEN

Cody was an intelligent woman. That was obvious. Ted was surprised when she told him that she never completed her college education. She'd left Ithaca following her junior year. Cody had only mentioned it in passing, but the therapist couldn't help but revisit the subject. That's when he learned Cody had quit school to be with Torrie Leeter.

Torrie's family owned a popular eatery in New York City's theatre district. Torrie spent a lot of time there when she was growing up. As a teenager she got to know many of the line dancers and showgirls who worked on Broadway.

It's no secret there are a lot of gays and lesbians in the theatre community. Both then and now. These days it's pretty much accepted, but back then show business was one of the only venues a person could be open about their sexual identity and still be employed. Torrie had just turned sixteen when one of the female line dancers invited her to attend *"a sewing circle."*

These so called *"sewing circles"* were groups of women who gathered together to pair up with members of their own gender. It is said the phrase comes from the quasi-secret sex parties held by some of Hollywood's 'A' list actresses back in the 1930s.

In Hollywood's golden years it was not uncommon for a popular actress to appear publicly with her leading man. Sometimes they even married them. It fed the flames of gossip and kept their names in the headlines. These so called *'lavender'* marriages were only a sham, hastily arranged for publicity. In truth many of Hollywood's best known actors and actresses were homosexuals leading double lives.

Torrie knew what she was getting herself into when she agreed to go to the sewing circle. The aging line dancer who invited her was notorious for going after young flesh. She certainly didn't have to talk Torrie into it. The pretty teenager went with eyes wide open.

For some reason Cody felt it necessary to provide her therapist with a detailed physical description of her one time lover. *"Torrie was tall and lean and well- muscled"* the dying woman bragged. *"She had beautiful big brown eyes and full lips. Torrie's only flaw was her nose. It was as wide as it was long."*

Ted could tell his patient still had strong feelings for this Torrie woman, even after all these years. The tone of her voice and the faraway look in her eyes told him so. He couldn't help but ask what happened to her.

"Torrie left me," Cody replied somewhat acerbically. The tone in her voice changed and the faraway look in her eyes disappeared. Ted figured maybe it would be a good idea to change the subject. Something in his question had opened up a long dormant wound. He was about to work his way out of that particular conversation when Cody suddenly carried it forward. She went on to tell her therapist all about the relationship the two women shared in the years following college.

They lived in a three room flat on the Lower East Side of Manhattan. The brownstone sat in the shadows of the Brooklyn

Bridge. Following World War II the Lower East Side was considered an affordable area for young people just starting out. That would change significantly in the decades to come.

According to Cody it didn't take long for her girlfriend to make a name for herself. She used the connections she'd made through her family's eatery to get her resume out to the theatre community. Within a week she was hired on as an executive assistant to a famous Broadway producer. A man named Boris Grayson.

Grayson was known far and wide for his ability to recognize good talent. He hired Torrie to help him manage a new musical he was producing. It was called *STORYVILLE*. The play went on to win several Tony Awards that year.

Storyville was set in turn of the century New Orleans. As the musical opens theatre goers find themselves sitting in a lavish house of ill repute known as *Sultry Sadie's*. Brothels were quite common in the French Quarter back then. They ranged from cheap cribs where a lady of the night could be had for fifty cents to elegant thirty room mansions that charged upscale clients ten dollars for the pleasure.

The actual Storyville District of New Orleans was established in the late 1800s by city officials wanting to regulate the practice of legalized prostitution. The intent was to limit the activity to a red light district where politicians could control the purse strings of those who set up shop.

They even had guides published to help visitors select which house of ill repute best suited their budgets and particular needs. These publications, deemed Blue Books, included descriptions of each bordello, as well as the prices each charged for services and what class of *"stock"* could be found there.

The district was adjacent to the city's main rail station making it relatively easy for visitors to find their way to the brothels. As Storyville's popularity grew dozens of drinking establishments began to pop up along its borders, opened by wily entrepreneurs ready and willing to accommodate the needs of the ever growing crowds. These saloons continued to operate even after legalized prostitution was banned by the city of New Orleans some twenty years later. Many remain open today.

With the outbreak of World War I local politicians came under the intense scrutiny of the United States government. The War Department had constructed a naval deployment center close to the Storyville District. The brass didn't want troops being sent off to fight a war to be distracted by what was going on right outside the deployment center's gates. As they say, all things must pass.

Grayson's play opened to rave reviews but due to contractual commitments with key members of his cast the production had a relatively short lifespan. In the seven and a half months it did run on Broadway *STORYVILLE* was seen by almost half a million people. That number happened to include Mr. Howard Hughes.

Hughes had recently purchased RKO Studios. He'd been in negotiations with Boris Grayson hoping to obtain the rights to 'STORYVILLE' so he could make it into a feature film. It was in those negotiations the wealthy tycoon heard about Grayson's executive assistant, Torrie Leeter. He made his way backstage after the performance hoping to meet her.

RKO Pictures had a long history of making quality films. Howard Hughes intended to continue that tradition. To do so he needed someone like Torrie to help him achieve his goal. He wanted her to come work for him in Hollywood. With Grayson's blessings she and Cody moved out of their Lower East Side flat the following week.

Torrie found immediate success working for Howard Hughes. Originally hired as the billionaire's personal assistant within a year she was promoted to executive producer. She and Cody bought a pricey bungalow in Hollywood Hills and started living the life. Torrie Leeter's name appears in the closing credits of no less than thirteen RKO productions. One of her films won a Golden Globe.

Torrie's successful film career came to an abrupt end several years later when she ended up on United States Senator Joe McCarthey's infamous blacklist. Someone at RKO Studios had anonymously identified her as a communist subversive. Without an inkling of proof Torrie was unceremoniously fired.

Rumors circulated around town saying it was Howard Hughes himself who provided the un-American Activities Committee with a list of RKO employees suspected of subversion. It was suggested he did so in order to clean house. Hughes wanted to rid himself of high salaried employees so he could sell the movie studio while it still had a brand name. Torrie's name was on that list.

It wasn't true of course. Torrie Leeter's only crime was liking girls. She was far from being alone in that regard. Half of Hollywood was queer. Still, being branded as a communist subversive took its toll. It made it impossible to find work in the industry Torrie had come to love. There wasn't a movie studio in Tinseltown that would touch her. God knows she tried.

Depression set in, helped along by drugs and alcohol. Cody told her therapist how she pleaded with her lover to get some counseling but the girl wouldn't listen. Torrie Leeter committed suicide the following year. Cody found her sitting naked on the toilet in an upstairs bathroom. She had sliced her wrist open with a butcher knife. Tears formed in the corners of Cody's eyes as she spoke the words.

Had Torrie Leeter held out a few more years she would have witnessed the passing of Senator Joe McCarthy. The republican demagogue who'd caused so much pain and suffering with his hate inspired assault on Hollywood was eventually castigated by his peers. In 1954 the senator was charged with contempt and abuse of power. He was found guilty and condemned by an overwhelming majority of the senate. Joe McCarthy died three years later. He was only forty-eight years old. It is said the shamed senator's abuse of alcohol played a role in his passing.

Cody told her therapist she wanted to celebrate the night she heard the news McCarthy had died. Many people did. The man was a blight on American society. His attacks were a constraint on liberty and justice and the human spirit. The enormous pain he caused was unjust and without merit. Perhaps God forgave him. Cody didn't think she could.

✝

CODY ROSE
CHAPTER EIGHT

Nearly seven years passed before Cody allowed herself to fall in love again. It wasn't planned, nor was she looking. It just sort of happened. Her name was Bobbie Evans and they met at a health food store in East Los Angeles.

Cody's symptoms were somewhat stable back then. She'd have minor setbacks, but nothing she couldn't cope with. To her credit Cody was trying to fight her illness holistically. That meant eating natural foods and taking naturopathic medications. Ingredients that came from Mother Earth. Bobbie Evans was very much into the holistic lifestyle as well.

Bobbie claimed she'd been a lesbian all her life. She insisted she was born that way. She had never even kissed a fella. Not even in high school. There was nothing about the woman that was feminine. That made for a very hard life. Back then it wasn't like it is today. In those days if you didn't hide your queerness you were ostracized for it.

Cody believed her new partner must have had some feminine attributes. All women do. She figured Bobbie just kept hers bottled up inside. That wasn't true. At her core Bobbie Evans was a male trapped in a woman's body. And like most males she could be a mistrusting and jealous person.

Those particular characteristics would not fully surface until some years later. Bobbie pretended to be a loving and protective partner for quite a while. Unfortunately she couldn't continue to personify someone she was not. In that way the relationship was doomed from the start. Despite how it ended Bobbie Evans was a positive force in Cody's life.

Take for example Cody's illness. Bobbie would have none of it. She convinced Cody her ailments were all in her head. The problem could be eliminated by adopting naturopathy as a way of life. To make her point she insisted the two of them leave L.A. and move someplace where Cody could take advantage of clean wholesome air and the suns healing powers.

Bobbie was convinced clean air and the rays of the sun played a central role in the naturopathic lifestyle. They were healing. The sun's warmth penetrating. The sun god was a deity that needed to be worshipped and meditated upon. Its rays were a vital source of energy. They held the power to transform one's inner spirit.

In the spring of 1962 the two women made the move. They'd researched their options and settled on Loving, New Mexico. Bobbie had some money saved up. She used nearly half of it to purchase a small two bedroom ranch in the town of Loving. Cody contributed what she could to the purchase but she had limited funds. Torrie had used up most of their assets fighting the un-American Ethics Committee.

Loving, New Mexico was a small town. Home to just over six hundred full time residents. Its citizens were mostly poor, mostly white, and mostly kept to themselves. Folks didn't seem to care what their neighbor down the street was doing as long as it didn't impact them. When two people settle down in a place like that they learn to rely on each other.

The town didn't offer much in the way of job opportunities. Least not back then. There was a small RV park situated along the banks of the Pecos River about three miles south of town that hired seasonal help. A hardware store in the center of town employed a handful of people, and there was a greasy spoon that had a half a dozen waitresses on their payroll. They were needed to feed the hungry truckers that passed through town on their way to what was left of the Carlsbad potash mines some twenty miles away.

At one time the potash mines were a major employer but those jobs started drying up in the early 1950's. The few that remained couldn't sustain the families that once depended on them for their sustenance. When the cutbacks came many left for greener pastures.

Things are different now. The area has grown by leaps and bounds in recent years. People have migrated there to work in the oil and natural gas facilities that sprang up along the Texas New Mexico border. The population has swelled. Urban sprawl from the city of Carlsbad has overflowed into neighboring towns like Loving. Cody wouldn't recognize the place today. It's not the same small town she moved to back in 1962.

It took a couple years but eventually the money Bobbie had saved started to dry up. She took up glass blowing as a way to generate income, using what remained of her savings to open a studio. After buying a furnace and the tools she needed to hone her gaffing skills she set out to master her craft. The woman became quite good at it.

Cody got a waitressing job down at the greasy spoon. That's when Bobbie's jealousy issues really started to surface. She became overly suspicious of her partner's interaction with her customers. Specifically the male truckers who stopped in for a meal and some conversation. Veiled threats and ugly innuendo soon followed.

It was foreseeable. Bobbie caught Cody in what she deemed uncompromising positions on several occasions. That fed fodder to the flames. One time she stumbled upon Cody sitting in the cab of some trucker's rig. Needless to say she went ballistic. Bobbie literally dragged her girlfriend out of the trucker's cab, all the while screaming for her to pack her stuff and go back to L.A. The altercation might have come to blows had Bobbie not quelled the situation by storming off.

If she had bothered to ask she would have discovered the trucker invited Cody to his cab to check out a batch of newborn puppies he had rescued from certain death. Someone had put them in a cardboard box and left them at a rest area along the highway. He was hoping to pawn one of them off. The little mongrels were fast asleep on the floor of his semi.

Another time Bobbie walked into the diner only to find Cody huddled in a corner booth talking with some trucker. The two of them were deep in conversation. Bobbie watched intently as Cody gazed into the trucker's eyes with tears rolling down her cheeks.

The sheriff had to be called on that one. When Bobbie saw the trucker wrap his arms around her partner she leaped across the table and attacked the poor guy. Fortunately for her he didn't fight back. He was at least twice her size. The trucker could have easily punched Bobbie's lights out. Instead he just blocked her blows until the cops arrived.

What Bobbie didn't know before she overreacted that day was that the trucker Cody was talking to was a man of God. He would often share his testimony with people he met on the road. The layman evangelist had led many a soul to Jesus. That's exactly what he was doing that day. Sharing the gospel with Cody.

She'd accepted. That was the reason for the tears. At the age of thirty-eight Cody Rose had become *"Born Again."* We're all familiar with the phrase. Everyone has been hounded at one time or another by some street preacher sternly warning us of the error of our ways. They try to frighten us with promises of impending doom unless we repent from our sins.

Some wave their leather bound bibles above their heads like they are weapons of war ready to split open the heads of those living in sin. This while simultaneously pleading for donations. They tell their audience they need the money to help spread the message of hope to the lost, but more than a few have been exposed as nothing more than thieves and charlatans.

This guy wasn't like that. The evangelizing trucker didn't preach damnation. He knew Cody was in a relationship with another woman but he didn't condemn her for it. He spoke words of love and acceptance and understanding. He didn't browbeat Cody with his bible. He simply offered a better way. And he didn't ask for a donation. He only asked that once Cody made a decision for Christ that she seek his voice and follow his direction.

Upon accepting Jesus Christ as Lord and Savior Cody knew she had to change her ways. What good is repentance if you don't? No one told her she had to break up with Bobbie. Cody could have remained in the relationship as if nothing had happened. The problem is it had. Cody was a new creation. To continue living her life as she had been would be counter to what she knew in her heart was right.

That didn't mean it was easy. Cody stuck around for a while. She stopped sleeping with her partner, and she tried to explain why she'd made the decision to repent. She shared the gospel with Bobbie in the hope she too would come to know the truth. It didn't happen.

It wasn't Bobbie's jealousy issues that caused the breakup. It was Cody's resurrection. Her partner rejected the bible as if it were an unwanted pregnancy. To a woman who identified herself as being male that is saying a lot. The idea she would consider becoming a Born Again Christian was aborted the moment the seed was planted.

Two months after accepting Christ Cody was on an airplane headed for the east coast. Florida to be exact. She told everyone she chose Florida because she'd always wanted to see the Atlantic Ocean and where better to see it than the Sunshine State? That was true, sort of. Cody did want to see the Atlantic Ocean, but the real reason she chose Florida was because of a dream she had.

In her dream Cody saw a man walking along the side of the road in front of her house. He was bundled up like it was the middle of winter in upstate New York. The man was wearing winter boots and an oversized parka, its fur lined hood pulled up high on his head. He looked very out of place in Loving, New Mexico.

Cody ran outside to ask the man why he was dressed like that but she got no answer. She then asked him where he was going. Again the fellow didn't answer. At least not verbally. He just pointed his hand northward and kept walking.

Frustrated, Cody called out for him to stop. **"Hold on a minute, Mister... Please wait up. I want to come with you."**

At that the man stopped dead in his tracks. After a short pause he turned and looked back at his pursuer. *"I have never turned anyone away"* he responded, *"but where my journey takes me you cannot go."*

Something very strange happened when the man turned to look back at Cody. The hood of his parka slid back on his shoulders to reveal he didn't have a face. At least Cody didn't see one. All she saw was a glowing. A soft shining light that seemed to glow inward.

Despite what she saw Cody wasn't frightened. She seemed to sense she was perfectly safe in his presence. *"Is it because I have dishonored my body that I cannot go,"* she asked?

The man replied, *"I know of no such thing. If that were true I would say so. The reason you cannot accompany me is because you have your own work to do. The garden needs tending."*

The man's comment made no sense to her. If there was one thing Cody did not have it was a green thumb. *"You need to plant seed in fertile soil, Cody Rose"* the man continued. *"Then water it and watch it grow."*

Cody looked down at the dry cracked earth between her feet and responded, *"But where am I to do this, Sir?"*

The man took a step forward before answering. When he did he inadvertently placed himself in the shadow of a large sassafras tree. At that moment Cody caught a glimpse of his face, now visible through the shadows. It lasted only a few seconds, but that was long enough. Cody realized she was in the presence of an angel. It was the most beautiful thing she had ever seen.

The angel glanced down at the ground beneath Cody's feet and held his gaze. Suddenly a flower sprang up out of the hard clay earth. A beautiful multi-colored flower with shimmering petals. *"Go to the land of flowers"* the angel replied. *"If we are to prepare a feast you must first tend the garden..."*

At that point Cody awoke from her dream. After a quick shower she jumped on her bike and pedaled down to the community library. The library was housed in an old refurbished office trailer that once sat on the site of Los Alamos Laboratories a few hours to the north. The feds donated the unit to the town of Loving after it had outlived its usefulness. There she found a set of encyclopedias.

Cody spent the better part of the afternoon pouring over those encyclopedias. It took a while but eventually she found what she was looking for. A reference to a place called *"The Land of Flowers."*

She learned that was the name Spanish explorer Ponce de Leon gave to the area of the New World he discovered in 1564. It is said when de Leon came ashore and saw the abundance of flowering plants along the shoreline he dropped down on his knees and thanked God, then proclaimed the land for the Spanish crown, calling it La Flora.

La Flora translates to Land of Flowers in English. De Leon had come ashore in what is now Florida. Cody took it as a sign. She was moving to the Sunshine State. The woman was on a mission. Sent there by an angel of God.

Cody arrived in Florida on September 11, 1964. Exactly four hundred and fifty years after Ponce de Leon's landing. She had been scheduled to fly into Jacksonville. Her plan was to rent a car and drive to Saint Augustine, about thirty miles to the south. Saint Augustine being the purported site of Ponce de Leon's landing in 1564. Unfortunately her flight was diverted to Orlando. A major hurricane had made landfall on the east coast of Florida the night before.

Hurricane Dora came ashore as a category three storm, with winds gusting up to one hundred and thirty miles per hour. The city of Saint Augustine was directly in its path. It wasn't quite the welcome Cody was hoping for. What were the chances? It had been sixty years since a hurricane hit that particular area of the state. Going there now was out of the question. Saint Augustine was half under water.

Cody found Orlando to be a diamond in the rough. The city was a fast growing jewel surrounded by wetlands and deserted orange groves. With the advent of central air conditioning the once sleepy town had become a winter haven for Northerners eager for a respite from the cold. By 1964 the sleepy burg had swelled to nearly 100,000 residents. Compared to Loving, population 608 minus 1, Orlando was heaven on earth.

Only a handful of people knew it at the time but Orlando was about to experience something that would forever change its future. Entertainment mogul Walt Disney was secretly preparing to purchase over 30,000 acres of what had once been orange grove country southwest of the city. A string of harsh winters had driven citrus growers to abandon the land they'd worked for so long. Most of them headed further south.

Disney had plans to build a theme park out there. They were kept secret for fear there would be a land grab and prices would soar if word got out. The planned theme park would far surpass his park in California in size and scope. Rumors had been running rampant for some time that something big was being planned for that giant parcel of land but no one foresaw what was to come.

Some suggested the land was going to be annexed by the State of Florida, with plans to build a future community out there. Lord knows one was needed. If real estate developers were going to accommodate the ever increasing number of retirees looking to move to Florida they had to have somewhere to put them all.

Others claimed the property was going be developed by the National Space Administration. America was preparing to put a man on the moon. The agency was expanding and more space was needed. The parcel of land Disney was secretly looking at was less than an hour from Cape Canaveral.

Some rumors suggested Lockheed Corporation was going to build a massive aircraft manufacturing plant out there. But they were all rumors. That parcel of land was spoken for. It was to become Disney World. The largest and most extravagant theme park on earth.

Unbeknownst to anyone outside his most inner circle Walt Disney had an even more ambitious project up his sleeve. Once his new theme park was up and running Walt wanted to build an experimental prototype city out there. EPCOT was to be a technologically advanced, residential friendly urban space. One in which people could live and work in harmony with their surroundings. It would be a model of American ingenuity, turning the most advanced ideas into reality. Disney's EPCOT would take humanity where it had only dreamed it could go. A true city of the future.

Unfortunately Walt Disney passed away before he could get his utopian venture off the ground. He never got to see his dream city become reality. No one did. After his death Disney executives decided to take the company in another direction. The EPCOT of today is not the futuristic City of Tomorrow that Walt Disney had envisioned. It's just another theme park.

✝

CODY ROSE
CHAPTER NINE

The 1960's were a tumultuous time in America. The decade was ushered in by the Cuban missile crisis, an act of Soviet aggression that brought our nation to the brink of nuclear war. That incident was closely followed by the assassination of President John F Kennedy, a slaying many still mourn today. As the decade came to a close it witnessed the murders of civil rights leader Martin Luther King, Jr and democratic Senator Robert Kennedy, who at the time was running for the office once held by his assassinated brother. Bobby was the odds on favorite to win the presidency.

Republican candidate Richard Nixon went on to claim a close victory in the election that year, winning out over Vice-President Hubert Humphrey. Nixon ran on a platform that promised to end the war in Vietnam and bring the troops home. The Vietnam War had become increasingly unpopular with voters. With visions of flag covered coffins being televised into people's living rooms on a nightly basis the war had lost much of its support.

Once he was in office the newly elected president did just the opposite. He expanded the nation's involvement in Vietnam, to the point of invading neighboring Cambodia. Nixon refused to be remembered as the first sitting president to ever "lose" a war. His decision to expand the war effort birthed a peace movement that would forever change the social and cultural landscape of the United States.

The sixties saw civil unrest run rampant across the nation. A generation of young blacks stood up to the racial inequality their predecessors had endured for centuries. Riots erupted in cities throughout the country as black people expressed their anger and frustration towards the injustices they experienced. Entire neighborhoods were engulfed in the flames of racial despair.

On college campuses antiwar demonstrators felt the sting of policeman's night sticks as peaceful rallies dissolved into chaos. Often times those whose job it was to protect the protesting students ended up inciting them instead. More times than not the National Guard had to be called in to restore order.

Inflation skyrocketed too, partially caused by a caustic federal government intent on spending hundreds of billions of taxpayer dollars to fight an unpopular war. Money earmarked for social programs put in place by the previous administration was diverted to the war effort. Programs like WIC and SSI paid the price. Not only were the Nation's poorest citizens being forced to fight a war, they were being forced to pay for it too.

Enter Cody Rose. She was on a mission from God. The recent convert came to Florida to plant seed, and plant she did. It started the moment she stepped off the airplane.

Cody was greeted on the tarmac by a black man in a military uniform. His name was Lt. Colonel Michael Greer. Greer was a United States Air Force test pilot stationed at nearby McCoy Air Base. McCoy being home to the 306th Bombardment Wing of the Strategic Air Command. When he saw Cody struggling with her bulky carry on Greer asked if he might be of assistance.

Together they made their way to the passenger terminal, which until recently had been a military hanger. The terminal still maintained much of the character of its former life. With the city of Orlando growing by leaps and bounds the old municipal airport just wasn't capable of handling the increased passenger traffic. When the United States Air Force offered to convert the hanger into a passenger terminal that the city could lease for pennies on the dollar they jumped at the chance.

The reason Lt. Colonel Greer was at the airport that day was to see off a very special friend of his. Civil rights leader Martin Luther King. King had come to Orlando to attend a Southern Baptist conference and to confer with the conference's guest speaker, the Reverend Billy Graham. King's plane was sitting on the tarmac right next to the one Cody had just gotten off.

Lt. Colonel Greer happened to be the son of a preacher himself. In fact King's father and his father were good friends. They both pastored large churches in the city of Atlanta, Georgia.

Upon reaching the terminal the Lt. Colonel suggested he and Cody grab a cup of coffee while she waited for the rest of her luggage. It would take a while for her suitcase to make its way to baggage claim. During their conversation Greer mentioned who he was seeing off that day. He went on to tell Cody he'd actually been named after Martin Luther King Jr's father.

That confused her. The famous civil rights leader was Martin, Jr. How then could this man claim he was named after King's father? Greer explained.

"Martin's father wasn't born Martin Luther King. His given name was Michael. The elder King changed his name to Martin Luther back in the 1930's after returning home from a trip to Germany"

While visiting Germany Pastor King became very interested in learning more about the protestant reformation movement. He knew German theologian Martin Luther was responsible for causing the split from Rome, but not much else. King was so inspired by Martin Luther's story he decided to honor him by taking his given name when he got back to America. When the pastor's son was born the name was passed on to him as well.

Cody was impressed. Her new friend was also good friends with Martin Luther King Jr. The man was the leader of the American civil rights movement. If Black people in America were going to demand the equality they were guaranteed under the United States Constitution they were going to need a spokesman to represent them. Martin Luther King Jr. was the right man at the right time.

Martin Luther King, Jr. had come to national prominence after being asked to intervene in a movement of civil disobedience that had sprung up in the city of Albany, Georgia some months before. Over five hundred black protestors had been jailed in the aftermath. When King interfered he ended up being arrested too. He was hauled off to jail along with an additional five hundred peaceful civil rights demonstrators who'd chosen to march with him.

With the total arrested at over one thousand the movement took on national importance. When word of King's arrest got back to Michael Greer's father he sent his son to bail him out. The two men had been close friends ever since.

Lt. Colonel Greer told Cody that Martin had introduced him to the Reverend Billy Graham the previous day, and that the two men had an interesting conversation. Greer was surprised to hear that the popular evangelist had himself been called upon to bail Martin Luther King, Jr. out of a jail on occasion.

The Reverend Billy Graham was fully committed to racial equality. All one had to do was attend one of his crusades to see that. Graham refused to hold segregated rallies, even in the Deep South. He would often tell his audience that the Lord Jesus Christ preached to all the peoples of the earth, and if it was good enough for Jesus it was good enough for him!

When Cody's baggage arrived Michael Greer offered to give her a lift to her final destination. Unfortunately Cody didn't have a final destination in mind. Her plan to settle in St Augustine having been thwarted by the hurricane. She had to tell her military escort her steps were being guided by God.

At that point Cody decided to tell Michael Greer about the dream she'd had back in New Mexico. She explained it was the realness of the vision that drove her to act. Being a born again believer himself the Lt. Colonel completely understood where she was coming from. He drove Cody to the local YWCA and got her a room.

Along the way he mentioned a buddy of his was hosting a dinner party at his home in Hillsborough County in a few weeks.

Greer asked Cody if she would consider being his date for the party.

Back in those days it was considered taboo for a black man to accompany a white woman on a date. Even one in full military regalia. It didn't matter that the two were born again Christians, or that Greer would never overstep the bounds of common decency. Cody was nearly bowled over when she learned the person hosting the dinner party was the Reverend Billy Graham.

Fortunately most of the guests attending the dinner party were accepting of a mixed race couple. Cody met quite a few notable people that night. Respected men of faith, as well as nationally recognized civil rights activists. A number of politicians were there too. People like future President Jimmy Carter. Back then Carter was just a Georgia State Senator, but one could tell he was destined for greatness.

Florida Congressman Charles Bennett was also in attendance. Bennett being the man responsible for introducing the bill that would make the words *'In God We Trust'* our national motto.

For a former lesbian from a small town in upstate New York this was truly high stepping. I mean who was she? A recent Christian convert who'd spent most of her adult life living counter to God's will. A college dropout with no job experience to speak of. A woman with a debilitating illness that could strike her down at any moment. Cody Rose was a Nobody. Those were the very words she used to describe herself to Billy Graham that evening. Of course he corrected her in no uncertain terms.

"God uses ordinary people in extraordinary ways, Ms. Rose," the popular evangelist preached. *"It is your humble nature that makes you the perfect candidate to do God's glory. Our Lord and Savior has great plans for you, young lady. You are not unworthy. Believe me… You will become a treasure to those you encounter, in Jesus' holy name."*

Reverend Graham went on to name a long list of people God has used to spread his message of hope. Folks who came from humble beginnings and tragic circumstances. People who, like Cody, would refer to themselves as being totally unworthy. Perhaps they were, until God came into their lives. He used them to accomplish mighty feats through the power of His grace.

Cody left that dinner party with a new sense of who she was in Christ, and what she was to accomplish. Her decision to move to Florida would not be in vain. From that point forward she would pick up her cross and march with her head held high. Cody Rose was a child of God, and He had given her a mission.

✝

CODY ROSE
CHAPTER TEN

Michael Greer was a graduate of the U.S. Air Force Academy. Upon graduation he was assigned to Griffiss Air Force Base in Rome, New York. The military test pilot had no idea then, but he was stationed only an hour's drive from Cody Rose's hometown.

Greer was part of the 27th Fighter-Interceptor Squadron. He flew F-89 Scorpions. The Scorpion was the first jet powered fighter in history to be armed with nuclear guided missiles. The young pilot never had to deliver his load, thanks be to God.

In 1959 Michael's entire unit was transferred to an air force base outside Boston, Massachusetts. He didn't make the trip. Greer and one other member of his unit had been selected for test pilot school. He was to report to Edwards Air Force Base located in Southern California.

The school had a rigorous advanced flight training program. Pilots were trained to evaluate new weapons systems and fly experimental aircraft. Only the best of the best got to attend. Michael was the first, and to that point the only black air force pilot to be so honored.

In the spring of 1963 Greer was transferred to McCoy Air Force Base in Orlando, Florida. McCoy had recently become a frontline Strategic Air Command Base. Test pilots were needed to test the upgraded B-52 Stratofortress. It was hoped the slimmed down bomber would give the Air Force improved stealth and guidance capabilities the older version of the plane could not. It was just too heavy for conventional use. That's how Greer came to be in Orlando when Cody arrived.

Three years to the day after their first meeting Lt. Colonel Greer was killed in the line of duty. He'd been performing a low altitude maneuver over the Atlantic Ocean when his plane broke apart. A subsequent internal investigation conducted by the air force determined the official cause of the crash to be structural fatigue. Too much stress had been put on the body of the aircraft. Low altitude flying had been an area of concern for flight engineers prior to Greer's flight, which was why Michael was testing it.

The accident forced the pentagon to look for ways to further improve the body of the airplane. Eventually a solution was found. A horizontal stabilizer was added to the rib cage of the plane's fuselage. This subtle change allowed for weight from the wings to be transferred to the stringers beneath the skin of the aircraft. That meant the B-52 could fly at lower altitudes. The newly improved bomber was used extensively in the years to come as America became entrenched in the war in Vietnam.

Ahhh yes... Vietnam. If ever there was a need for prayer it was then. The country was in turmoil. Television news crews embedded with American troops aired footage of the atrocities being committed in Southeast Asia on a nightly basis. The war had divided the nation. A nation which was already struggling with the issue of racial inequality. After the assassinations of Robert Kennedy and Martin Luther King Jr. there was a tidal wave of political unrest.

People were scared. The parents of the Vietnam generation had lost the ability to communicate with their children. They looked on in silent horror as America's sons and daughters demonstrated in the streets. Lyndon Baines Johnson had taken over when John Kennedy was assassinated. As his term came to a close he decided to throw in the towel and not run for reelection.

The man who gave us the Civil Rights Act, the Voting Rights Act, and much needed immigration reform could not handle the immense heat of an internal combustion engine out of control. A president who singlehandedly helped millions of American citizens climb out of the clutches of poverty with his *'New Deal'* could not stay the course. LBJ's decision not to run led to the election of Richard Nixon.

Cody Rose wasn't part of this new breed of demonstrator. She'd been a child of the *'Beat Generation'*. A follower of Jack Kerouac and Allen Ginsburg. One a victim of alcoholism, and the other of drug abuse. It was only natural that she continue her ways into middle age.

By 1968 Cody was working as a manager for a nonprofit entity called the Community Housing Fund. CHF was a consortium of concerned citizens that took control of once abandoned buildings and refurbished them into small apartments. They then rented the spaces out to needy tenants using a sliding scale.

Many of the boarders were young people who'd dropped out of college to follow whatever passion they felt compelled to follow. Some were unemployed war veterans suffering combat stress disorder. Cody was adamant that none of the tenants bring drugs or alcohol into any facility she managed.

Because she was older than most of her tenants Cody was looked up to as being a wise lady. She insisted that the people living in her buildings interact with one another. Residents were expected to support one other like a family. They paid what they could for their accommodations. In many cases there was no set price. Cody insisted the Lord would provide.

Eventually Cody was chosen to be the new administrator of the consortium. Her lack of a college degree was superseded by her strong work ethic and obvious compassion for the tenants. Getting that job was a dream come true for Cody. It gave her a connection to outside resources she never would have had without being in that position.

As the year was ending another one of Cody's dreams was fulfilled when America's space program put a manned capsule in orbit around the moon. Astronauts Frank Borman, Jim Lovell, and William Anders became the first humans to see the dark side of the moon.

The moment was forever embedded in Cody's heart when the crew of Apollo 8 addressed the world on live television. Bill Anders was the first to speak. *"We are now approaching lunar sunrise,"* he told his captivated audience of millions back on earth. The astronaut then proceeded to read from the holy bible.

"In the beginning God created heaven and earth. And the earth was without form, and void. Darkness was on the face of the deep. And the Spirit of God moved upon the waters, and God said

"LET THERE BE LIGHT" and there was light. God saw the light, that it was good. He divided the light from the darkness."

Each of the other two astronauts then took turns quoting from the scripture, with Frank Borman closing it out by reading verses nine and ten. He followed up by wishing everyone back home a Merry Christmas. Once the cameras were turned off the three space travelers joined hands and prayed. They asked God to bring peace and good will to all nations.

NASA's space program successfully accomplished its ultimate mission seven months later when Neil Armstrong stepped foot on the surface of the moon. The first human being to do so. *"One small step for man. One giant leap for mankind."* That mission would be followed by six more flights to the lunar surface. Five of them were successful. The one failure being Apollo 13.

What's odd about that fact is that of all the flights NASA sent into space it is Apollo 13 the agency is most proud of. The fact they were able to bring all three astronauts home safely after an on board explosion was nothing short of miraculous. Cody Rose would refer to the wondrous accomplishment this way. *"It was God...just doing his God thing. Plain and simple."*

The next few years would see the nation face more trauma. In the spring of 1970 the United States Congress established a national draft lottery that allowed the federal government to selectively force men into the military by using a numbers scheme. It proved to be a flawed system because the odds of being selected were not the same for everyone. Besides that, people of wealth and prominence were often able to avoid being drafted for obviously false reasons. All one need do was hire an expensive lawyer or bribe a doctor to lie about their medical condition. The backlash only strengthened the anti-war effort being played out on nearly every college campus in the land.

One night Cody had a second Spirit filled dream. Like the one she had in New Mexico many years before this dream also involved a mysterious man. The man was suffering terrible bouts of grief. His body was literally riddled with anguish. It was debilitating in that the man could not function, most especially in his job, which was of some importance. Oddly the man's pain came not from within, but from without.

The Lord showed Cody that the anguish the man was feeling was the pain of humanity laid at his feet. He was being forced to deal with it as if it were his own. The poor fellow was saddled with all this grief because in many ways he was responsible for it. He had inflicted pain on others by way of the decisions he had made. Those decisions were now coming home to roost.

The man in Cody's dream had once been a man of elevated stature, blessed with all the gifts he needed to succeed at the highest level. He had at one time believed in God, but he'd allowed his pride get in the way of his faith. The Lord gave Cody a word of knowledge for this man, with instructions to share it with him when confronted.

The Lord's words were these…***"Pride goes before destruction, and a haughty spirit before stumbling."*** Cody was to find this man and share with him these words the Lord had given her.

But who was this person? Who was she to seek out? Cody was not a wealthy woman, nor was she well connected. She didn't inhabit the land of plenty. Truth is she survived on a relatively meager income. Cody wasn't knowledgeable on matters of great importance, nor was she overly confidant in her ability to change someone's opinion. Rather than dwell on the dream Cody put it in God's hands. When He was ready it would be revealed.

Cody was good at one thing. She knew how to plead her case, and she had a case to plead. She wanted the war in Vietnam to end. She wanted those soldiers brought back home where they belonged. Cody knew she could open doors where others had failed. She just needed someone of authority to get her to that door.

That meant finding a person of power and influence who would understand her commitment. That someone was future President of the United States Jimmy Carter.

Carter was running for Governor in his home state of Georgia. He was expected to win the election in a landslide. There was already talk circulating around Washington that the popular politician was considering a future run at a national office.

Cody had made a good impression on Jimmy Carter when they met at that dinner party hosted by Billy Graham years before. She decided to send him a letter asking if he might consider speaking to the mayor of Orlando on her behalf. Cody wanted to organize a peace rally in downtown Orlando. She would need the approval of the city's mayor.

Mayor Langford had been in office for quite a few years. He is credited with bringing the city of Orlando into the future, having become mayor at the same time Walt Disney was deciding to build his new theme park in the abandoned orange groves southwest of the city.

Langford had a reputation for enjoying the limelight. When Disney came to town others soon followed in his footsteps. A number of big name Hollywood movie producers set up shop, as did a swell of corporate leaders. Folks Langford could rub elbows with. Democrat or not the mayor had no use for the counter-culture gurus who wanted to upset his applecart. Nor those who stood with them.

Jimmy Carter contacted Cody the moment he received her letter. Certainly he remembered her. She was the little lady with the big heart he spoke to at Billy Graham's dinner party. He'd been very impressed with her. Carter told Cody that he often wondered what became of her. He actually referred to her as *"An American Mother Theresa."*

Now that was stretching it. Cody Rose was in the business of doing God's work, but on a much smaller scale than that of Mother Theresa. The future winner of the Nobel Peace Prize had started soup kitchens and opened dispensaries in the heart of Calcutta. She'd arranged for health clinics to provide free medical care to the poor. Orphanages to house parentless children, many of whom were being taken advantage of in the worst possible way by men on the street. Cody was no Mother Theresa, but she did care about people.

Jimmy Carter said he would be glad to help. In fact he'd do more than just give the mayor of Orlando a phone call. He would pay him a personal visit. It would have to wait until after the election, but Carter was willing. Certainly an impromptu visit from the sitting governor of a neighboring state would be welcomed. Besides he was a Southern Baptist, just like Langford.

Carter made good on his promise. He showed up at Orlando City Hall some months later, however his request for an audience with the mayor was summarily snubbed. Evidently word of his impending rise within the ranks of the DNC had not reached Mayor Langford. He had his secretary tell the governor the mayor was too busy preparing a speech he was giving at the opening ceremonies of Walt Disney World to be interrupted.

Of course that wasn't true. The theme park wasn't scheduled to open for several more months. Mayor Langford knew the political leanings of the ultraconservative Disney family. Despite Walt Disney's untimely passing he still had to contend with his older brother, Roy. Langford wasn't about to have a private audience with a left leaning liberal Governor. Even if he was from a neighboring state.

Roy Disney had taken control of his brother's company upon his death. Like Walt, he was politically speaking a right wing extremist. Roy Disney despised the Democratic Party, believing they were nothing more than a guise for communism. Some have claimed the Disney brothers were staunchly anti-Semitic, pointing to their German heritage and close ties to United States Senator Joe McCarthey. Blasphemy, I know.

There was no way Mayor Langford was going to mess with the status quo. Democrat or not, Southern Baptist or not, there would be no lunching with Jimmy Carter. Did the newly elected governor from Georgia realize how much money the Vietnam War was generating? Langford was trying to woo large defense contractors to the area. Those companies employed thousands of people and paid high wages. The last thing he wanted was some sniveling anti-war protestors demonstrating in his back yard.

Not to be outdone Carter did an end around worthy of an NFL highlight reel. He contacted his good friend, the Reverend Billy Graham.

Billy recalled meeting Cody Rose at his dinner party too. She was the young lady that had accompanied Lt. Colonel Michael Greer that night. He remembered the gleam in her eye and the passion in her voice as she spoke. Graham had been convinced that one day Cody would do great works for the Lord.

With the exception of JFK who was a Catholic, Billy Graham had been a spiritual advisor to every American president since Harry Truman. He was good friends with Dwight Eisenhower and very close to Lyndon Johnson. LBJ conferred with Graham on nearly everything. It is a little known fact that Billy Graham had his own bedroom in the Johnson White House. That tells you how often he must have stayed there.

President Richard Nixon also sought Billy Graham's counsel on matters of State. He knew the evangelist well, having been Vice-President under Eisenhower. One time Nixon invited Graham to the oval office to discuss a course of action he was about to implement. It had to do with the war effort.

Back then one could only speculate on what advice Billy Graham may have given the president. Of course nowadays much of the truth has come out thanks to the Freedom of

Information Act. Whatever was said in that meeting, the following day Richard Nixon ordered the bombing of communist held sanctuaries in both Laos and Cambodia. The president's unconscionable act only served to extend the war.

It is worth noting that at one point in his presidency Richard Nixon actually offered Billy Graham an ambassadorship. The famous evangelist could have been the U.S. ambassador to Israel. Graham politely declined. After all he was a minister of the word, not a politician.

Reverend Billy Graham was one of the most admired men in America and Jimmy Carter knew it. One would be hard pressed to deny him a request, no matter its cause.

When Jimmy Carter approached Billy Graham with Cody's request he was told such a request would normally not even be considered. The evangelist said it was his belief that the peace movement in America was backed and supported by communist influence. The only reason he might agree to speak to Mayor Langford on Carter's behalf was because he admired Cody so much.

CODY ROSE
CHAPTER ELEVEN

It took Cody months of preparation but on New Year's Day 1969 *The Orlando Rally for Peace* finally happened. An estimated quarter million people showed up on the banks of Lake Nona in downtown Orlando to celebrate their unity and demand an end to the war in Vietnam. In truth the rally was more like a festival than an anti-war demonstration. Good vibes filled the air. Cody could not have been any happier or more proud of those in attendance.

Billy Graham had been able to convince the city's mayor that the rally would be good for his reelection efforts, reminding him war protesters vote too. Besides, he was planning to speak to the crowd himself. He planned to tell all who would listen about Jesus Christ and the sacrifice that was made for them. Graham was well aware of the fact most Americans wanted out of Vietnam. Despite his hawkish leanings the famous evangelist had to agree with them. The war had gone on long enough.

When Langford heard he would be rubbing elbows with some of the biggest names in show business it helped seal the deal. Graham convinced the mayor he would be seen as a hip forward thinking politician. Now that Disney World was up and running he didn't have to worry so much about pissing off Roy Disney. The theme park was immensely successful. He knew the Disney folks weren't going anywhere.

Cody had managed to recruit an A-list celebrity to headline the event. Academy Award winning actor Darrin Sheedy. Sheedy was

Hollywood's most outspoken critic of the war in Vietnam. He didn't just talk about his opposition either. The famous actor got involved. Darrin had made dozens of public appearances with politicians, so long as they opposed the war. To this day the popular actor is a work horse for progressives seeking office.

The event received nationwide exposure. All three television networks covered it, as did the nation's major newspapers. The list of celebrities helped. Sheedy had gone to his war chest and come up with some big names to appear on stage with him. The charismatic actor had friends throughout the entertainment industry. One person not on the official roster of scheduled speakers was Georgia Governor Jimmy Carter. He spoke anyway.

During a lull in the program Carter side straddled his way onto the stage and made his way up to the podium. He grabbed the microphone before anyone knew what was happening and started to speak. The governor was relatively unknown outside his home state of Georgia. Most of the country had never heard of him yet.

He finger tapped the mic a few times to test it, then in his rural Georgia peanut farmer accent said, *"Is this thing on? Can you all hear me out there?"* The governor had a shit eating grin on his face as he spoke the words. It made it hard not to like him. *"Good afternoon, Folks"* he bellowed. *"My name is Jimmy Carter."*

The crowd seemed a bit apprehensive at first. Who was this guy? Carter stood there on stage wearing baggy carpenter pants and a checkered shirt buttoned up to the collar? He looked like a cross between Howdy Doody and Captain Kangaroo.

"Many of you don't know me. I am the newly elected governor of the great state of Georgia, and I appreciate your listenin to what it is I got to say...."

A hush came over the crowd as Carter continued. *"Now I know I don't appear on the roster of official speakers, but I think it's important we talk about some things. First off let me give you all some background information. I attended the U.S. Naval Academy up in Annapolis, Maryland."*

Carter's comment drew an immediate groan from the crowd. He ignored it and continued his spiel. *"Upon graduation I served on the nuclear submarine USS SEAWOLF under Admiral Hyman Rickover. Of course the admiral was only a captain back then,"* he joked.

There was a spattering of laughter from the crowd this time. Carter went on say he was proud to have served in the navy, and that the experience taught him a valuable lesson. Namely that the United States of America needs to actively seek a nuclear proliferation agreement with the Soviet Union.

That comment got the crowd's attention and drew lots of cheers. Carter explained why he felt that way. He told the crowd that he had been part of a team of specialists who were sent in to clean up a spill aboard a submarine after a nuclear reactor suffered a serious meltdown. Millions of gallons of radioactive waste had flooded the reactor's inner core. The results could have been catastrophic.

"It is vitally important that our government cease developing nuclear weapons," Carter insisted. *"Ladies and gentlemen, the future of the world depends on it."*

This time the governor's comments drew raucous applause. Perhaps that is what inspired him to continue, though on a completely different subject. He told the huge throng the first thing he did when he was elected governor of Georgia was to publicly declare that the time of racial segregation in his state was over. *"No black person in Georgia shall ever again be deprived the opportunity to get an education, hold a job, or achieve simple justice."*

This pronouncement drew an even louder response than his previous one. Then the governor changed course yet again. This time addressing the Vietnam War. He called for the Nixon Administration to announce an immediate cease fire and a roll back of troops. The roar from the crowd was deafening. The future president ended his diatribe by calling Cody Rose to the dais.

Carter introduced Cody as being the person solely responsible for making this event happen. *"We all owe her a debt of gratitude,"* the governor pronounced. *"Ms. Rose is one of you all. She's a local girl. Cody runs a not for profit housing consortium right here in the city of Orlando. She loves people... and just like all of us, she wants to end this God dang war!"*

The crowd loved it. After basking in the glory for a moment Carter handed the mic to Cody and encouraged her to step up to the podium. After a moment she did.

"Thank you, Governor Carter" Cody said as she came forward. "We all sure hope you run for President some day!" She turned to the crowd and shouted, **"DON'T WE ORLANDO?"**

It was the perfect response. The crowd cheered long and loud. When the applause died down Cody got serious. "*I want to thank everyone for coming out today. Thank you so much for caring about our great nation. We are a nation founded on principles. We are one nation under God...and we love Jesus.*"

She went on to thank Billy Graham. "*This event would not have happened without you. Come out and take a bow, Reverend.*" With that Cody put her hands together and clapped along with the huge crowd as Billy Graham waved from the wings. This was not turning out as he envisioned. He was used to masses of people falling on their knees and repenting. These people were smoking pot and chanting antiwar slogans.

Cody continued. "*I would be remiss if I didn't mention the mayor. Mayor Langford allowed us to congregate here in this beautiful park today. Thank you, Mr. Mayor.*"

She started to place the microphone back in its stand then thought better of it and pulled it back. Cody waved her arm in a big semicircle and hollered, **"*I almost forgot. I want to send a heartfelt thank you to all the men in blue protecting us here today. Thank you, Guys. You are doing a wonderful job. We are so proud of you. This ain't Chicago!*"**

Cody looked out at the crowd and shrugged. "*I promised if we were allowed to gather here today we would hold a peaceful demonstration. We didn't want a scene like what happened at the convention in Chicago. That was a disaster. You are with me on that, right guys?"*

Cody went on to explain the reason she wanted to hold the rally, and what she was hoping it would accomplish. Her words came from the heart.

"Life is precious brothers and sisters. Everyone's life is. Red and yellow, black and white. We are all precious in His sight. No one knows the hour or the day Jesus will return. That is for the Lord to decide. All we can do is be the best that we can be. I pray all the time, and I ask God to soften President Nixon's heart. Too many lives have been lost. We are taught to love one another, and treat others as we would want to be treated. It is our faith in God that makes our nation strong."

One of the television network camera operators zoomed in on Cody's face as she spoke. She looked directly into the lens and said, *"It is time you bring our young men home, Mr. President."*

With that Cody placed the microphone down on the lectern and joined Governor Carter. He put his arm around her shoulder and the two started toward the wings of the stage. As they did Cody heard a number of people in the crowd start to sing. It was the perfect song for that moment in time. John Lennon's antiwar anthem, *'Give Peace a Chance.'*

Moments later the entire throng joined in. All two hundred and fifty thousand of them. You could hear the famous Beatle's words ricocheting off of Orlando's office building walls and down the avenues. *"All we are saying... Is give peace a chance..."* The verse John wrote was simple and repetitive but it spoke for a generation.

Cody turned and walked back to the podium. She looked out at the sea of people swaying back and forth, their arms locked in unison. An army of long haired, bell bottomed peaceniks all singing John Lennon's lyrics with tears of joy rolling down their cheeks. It was a beautiful sight to behold.

The crowd continued singing for twenty minutes at least. Television cameras caught it all. The moment was broadcast to tens of millions of viewers across the country. Because it was New Year's Day many people were sitting in their living rooms gathered around their television sets watching the Rose Bowl football game. The network interrupted the game to show its viewers what was happening in Orlando.

President Nixon happened to be in the White House watching the game that day. Being a native of California he was rooting for USC and their star running back O.J. Simpson. The game was tied when the decision was made to interrupt the broadcast.

It is said the president threw a temper tantrum that would have made a preschooler proud. He started cussing and fussing like a damn fool, slamming his glass down on the curved wooden arm of his easy chair. The contents splattered across the front of his white dress shirt, only making matters worse.

Nixon was so upset he threatened to phone the play by play announcers in the booth and order them to resume the telecast. The news correspondent on the scene in Orlando didn't help matters when he commented on air, *"President Nixon is going to go bonkers when he sees this!"*

Richard Nixon stood seething as he gazed at his television screen. Finally he bellowed, *"Those Fucking long haired hippies are going to ruin this country someday. Goddamn communists."*

Once the president regained his composure he walked over to a side table and made himself another drink. His favorite recipe was an equal mix of whiskey and gin with a dash of peach bitters on the rocks. The concoction was actually called 'The Nixon'. After slamming it down the president went to the oval office. Later that evening he made a phone call. It took several rings before the person he was trying to reach picked up the telephone.

"Bill.... Reverend Graham... Hello, this is Dick... Yes, Dick Nixon. Are you alone? Can you talk?"

The president told his spiritual advisor he had been watching the Rose Bowl football game that afternoon when the network suddenly switched their signal so they could cover the antiwar demonstration down in Orlando. **"It surprised the hell out of me when I saw you on my television screen,"** Nixon bellowed into the receiver. **"What the hell is going on down there, Reverend? How the hell did you get yourself involved in that damned foolishness...and why are you standing next to that Goddamn actor? That Sheedy fellow is a damn communist."**

Graham reminded the president he was talking to a man of God, then tried to explain what had gone on. He told him not to worry. The rally was over and things would soon return to normal. *"The kids were holding a peace rally, Dick. It wasn't what I would call a demonstration. They pretty much behaved themselves, although some of them could have used a bath and a haircut. Mayor Langford let them hold it in the park. He is a democrat you know."*

The president had calmed down considerably. He asked his spiritual advisor a rather odd question. He wanted to know who the young lady was he saw on stage addressing the crowd. President Nixon said he was impressed with how she conducted herself and he seemed anxious to know her story. The reverend filled him in.

Graham told the president the girl's name was Cody Rose, and that she was a true firebrand. *"Cody got saved a few years back, Dick. It changed her life. She was living as a lesbian but she has repented. She is a Spirit filled Born Again Believer, Mr. President. I would love for you to meet her some time. You would be impressed. That I can promise you."*

✝

CODY ROSE
CHAPTER TWELVE

By the spring of 1971 America's ground troops were doing the brunt of the fighting in South Vietnam. Folks back home were subjected to disturbing images of flag draped caskets sitting on tarmacs awaiting transport home on a nightly basis. The nation groaned in unison as the latest casualty figures appeared on America's television screens.

These images contrasted sharply with those of anti-war demonstrators wreaking havoc on college campuses throughout the land. The Vietnam War had become increasingly unpopular. Nixon's top political aides knew something had to be done to stop the hemorrhaging. Several of them urged the president to reduce the number of ground troops and replace them with firepower from above instead.

Up to that point the United States Air Force had been limited to providing support cover for combat troops. That and clearing out landing zones for the 1st Cavalry. Nearly 400,000 tons of napalm had been used to accomplish that feat.

Massive bombing runs like those waged against Nazi Germany was deemed futile by President Nixon's military commanders. They understood that dropping twenty megaton bombs on a country with limited infrastructure would only serve to kill large numbers of the civilian population. Nixon didn't listen.

His civilian advisors were able to convince him that it made sense to bomb the North Vietnamese into oblivion. High ranking staffers argued that a war waged from on high would ultimately save American lives.

The same argument had been made to convince Harry Truman to drop the atomic bomb on Hiroshima. As in that case, the argument was not based on fact. The real reason the United States dropped the atomic bomb on Japan was to instill fear in the hearts of the Soviet Union. The allies were convinced Stalin would try to force his influence on how Europe would be divided once the war was over. The Soviet dictator was much less likely to exert pressure knowing America had developed a nuclear weapon.

The military industrial complex that grew out of the war effort made huge fortunes for American corporations. These industrial giants supplied the government with everything they needed to wage war. From the planes and jeeps, to the oil needed to run them. In order to keep their cash cow's heart pumping there had to be a viable threat hanging over America, and it had to be threatening enough to allow them to continue producing their weapons of war in ever increasing numbers. That threat was the Russians.

The Soviet threat was over embellished to the newly installed president. Truman had been in office just three months when the decision was made to drop the bomb.

Many people don't realize it but Harry Truman was only in line to become president because FDR was pressured into taking him as his running mate during the presidential election of 1944. Henry Wallace had been Roosevelt's running mate for his first two terms in office.

At the Democratic Convention that summer Right leaning Southern Democrats got together and demanded Henry Wallace be taken off the ticket. He was far too liberal for their liking. The man was known to prefer conciliation with the Soviets once the war was over. Pushed on by corporate power brokers they lobbied Roosevelt to replace his vice-president with Missouri congressman Harry Truman. Someone they thought they could control. Not wanting to split the party while the country was at war Roosevelt conceded.

It was a deceptive move motivated by greed and power. It was no secret that FDR was in declining health. Once Roosevelt was out of the way Truman would have no choice but to rely on the corporate power brokers who put him there. The one term congressman was simply unprepared to make sound decisions for the country.

What resulted from all these political shenanigans was what the corporate power brokers wanted all along. A race for military supremacy with the Soviet Union. As the two countries built up their defensive capabilities America's military industrial complex flourished.

The decision to drop an atomic bomb on Japan was based on nothing more than cold hard cash. Truth is that by the spring of 1945 the Japanese were all but defeated. A declaration of surrender was already being negotiated between Hirohito and the allies. Roosevelt and Churchill were in agreement. Only Josef Stalin's signature was needed to end the war.

The sticking point was Stalin's insistence that Emperor Hirohito not remain in power after the war. Many believe Stalin was only stalling for time so that Soviet troops could be relocated from the Western Front to the Far East. With the Nazi's defeated the Soviet dictator had set his sights on the Korean Peninsula. Knowing this the power brokers controlling President Truman convinced him the time had come for America to act in her best interest. On August 6th 1945 the order to drop the atomic bomb was given.

One hundred and forty thousand people died as a result of the blast. Three days later a second bomb was dropped on the city of Nagasaki. The corporate power brokers got their wish. The love of money truly is the root of all evil...

And so it was with America's bombing of North Vietnam. It was seen as a ruthless act of cowardice. Destroying villages full of innocent civilians and taking out roads and bridges hurt the country's general populace far more than it did the government of North Vietnamese. Twenty years of continuous fighting had given the enemy plenty of time to build an elaborate network of underground tunnels. Nixon's bombs couldn't touch them.

That didn't stop him. It seemed the more his decisions were met with ridicule at home the more the president insisted on extending the conflict, no matter how unattainable winning the war might be.

Nixon simply failed to understand that winning was not going to be possible. He didn't even have the support of his own troops, most of whom were draftees sent to Vietnam against their will. Did he really think those young men wanted to die just so he could save face?

When the decision to carpet bomb North Vietnam was first discussed the president summoned Billy Graham to the White House. Nixon valued the preacher's input. It didn't become public until years later that Reverend Graham actually supported the president's decision to bomb the daylights out of North Vietnam. In fact data released through the Freedom of Information Act shows Graham was the one who suggested Nixon bomb the dikes surrounding the capital city of Hanoi.

The preacher's suggestion was never carried out. Doing so would have destroyed the agricultural system of North Vietnam. There would have been massive food shortages. An already suffering civilian population would have starved to death had Graham's advice been followed.

The president did target other civilian installations though. Nixon saved the heaviest bombing for the Christmas Holidays. That's when he called for the total destruction of Hanoi.

For twelve days leading up to Christmas 1972 enough bombs rained down on the North Vietnamese capital to reduce it to rubble. It has been said those twelve days of devastation were the most concentrated military bombing effort in world history.

At the same time America was carpet bombing the capital of North Vietnam officials from both countries were conducting peace talks in Paris. Not surprisingly those talks fell apart. It would be over a year before the two sides would come together again to try to end the conflict. Nixon used that time to escalate a secret offensive he'd started against another perceived enemy. This time the leadership of the Democratic Party.

Paid for with funds diverted from his re-election campaign the president's offensive was aimed at Democratic congressional candidates seeking reelection. Many prominent politicians came under intense scrutiny, as did members of their families.

It was a crusade of underhanded debauchery the likes of which this country had never seen. Of course we all know how that turned out. Richard Nixon's dirty tricks campaign was eventually shut down. The scandal would bring the president's proverbial house of cards crashing down around him. No less than forty high ranking government officials were sent to jail. The list included the Attorney General of the United States, along with Nixon's Chief of Staff, his personal assistant, and his Special Counsel.

The president himself was not jailed, but he was forced out of office. With the certainty of impeachment hanging like a noose around his neck Nixon left in disgrace a year and a half into his second term. President Gerald Ford issued his predecessor a full pardon upon taking over the presidency.

Dick Nixon would continue to defend his actions long after he was shown the door. The poor man just couldn't come to terms with his failures…

In the midst of all that mess President Nixon invited Cody to come to Washington for a visit. One day she was sitting behind her desk quietly reviewing rental applications when a man in black appeared at her door. The secret service man held in his hand an envelope bearing the presidential seal.

She was invited to join the commander in chief for a private luncheon at a yet to be named restaurant in the Georgetown section of D.C. All of her travel expenses would be covered.

How do you say no to the leader of the free world? Cody arranged her schedule so she could attend the luncheon. She even went shopping for a new dress. This would be her first trip to the nation's capital. She really didn't know what to expect.

Why would the President of the United States want to meet her? It had to have something to do with the peace rally she'd organized three years ago. Was she in trouble? The Orlando event had gone off without incident. Even the mayor and police chief acknowledged that.

It had to be Billy Graham's doing. The famous evangelist was a close confidant of Richard Nixon. He must have arranged the meeting. But why? What could she possibly say to President Nixon that would sway him one way or the other on any subject?

Perhaps she was getting ahead of herself. Cody didn't even know if she would have a chance to converse with the president. She'd simply been invited to attend a luncheon. For all she knew there would be dozens of people there.

Cody flew in to Reagan International Airport the night before. The government was putting her up at *The Casements,* a five star hotel located in Foggy Bottom. The next morning she was awakened by a bellhop. He was holding in his hand one of those plain white envelopes with the presidential seal.

The envelope contained a handwritten note. It simply stated an address and a time. *The 1776 - 36th Street NW - 12:00 noon.*

The sky was overcast with temperatures in the low fifties when Cody climbed out of her cab and stood on the sidewalk outside the restaurant. *The 1776* was located in a two hundred year old structure with large stained glass windows that depicted scenes of the American Revolution. An enormous American flag flapped in the breeze above the main entrance.

Cody had arrived early on purpose. Far be it from her to show up late for lunch with the President of the United States. As she stood waiting outside the restaurant she thought she sensed something sinister in the cool morning air. It lingered there like the smell of spilled gasoline. Cody couldn't put her finger on it, but she hoped nobody would light a match.

Despite the dire feeling she decided to kill some time by taking a stroll. A few minutes later Cody found herself standing outside a Catholic church. She'd stopped to admire the church's baroque architecture. She was about to continue her journey when a priest walked out of the multi arched front entrance. The two struck up a conversation.

The priest told Cody all about the church's fabled history. She learned it once claimed President John Fitzgerald Kennedy as a member. The assassinated president routinely attended services there when he was in D.C. Cody didn't mention she was having lunch with a president herself that day. She had been instructed not to. The meeting was private, as was the location.

As she made her way back towards the restaurant Cody saw a shiny black limousine pull up to the front entrance. A spiffily dressed chauffer exited the vehicle and made his way around to the passenger side. In the meantime a second car carrying two men in black suits pulled in behind the limo. One of the men hopped out and approached the chauffer. After he'd given his all clear the chauffer opened the rear door of the limo and a familiar face stepped out onto the sidewalk.

Billy Graham had seen Cody walking down the street as he was approaching. He held his gaze until she reached him, then took her hand. Graham apologized for being a tad late, even though he wasn't.

They were about to enter the restaurant when a group of people came bounding out the door. One of them was a priest, his cassock and clerical collar a dead giveaway. When the priest realized who he had just stumbled upon he stopped dead in his tracks.

"Reverend Graham," he said. *"What a pleasant surprise."* The look in the elderly priest's eyes suggested he didn't really find the chance meeting all that pleasant.

"Father Murphy," Graham responded. *"The pleasure is all mine, praise God. Did I hear you are appearing in a movie they've been shooting in town? Something to do with exorcism?*

The priest acknowledged Graham's comments, explaining he was asked to be a spiritual consultant for the film, *"Much like you with your presidents,"* he added. Then the old priest leaned forward and whispered over his spectacles, *"Tell me Reverend, how's that going these days?"*

The movie Graham was referring to was *The Exorcist.* Many of the controversial films scenes were being shot at a location just down the street from the restaurant. When Cody heard that she knew she would have to go see the movie when it came out in theatres. It was not a film Cody wished to see twice.

The maître d greeted Reverend Graham and his guest as they entered, then escorted them to a private dining room towards the back of the restaurant. Though the room was quite small it was very well appointed. A burly man dressed all in black stood guard outside the doorway. Cody entered first. As she did Richard Nixon put his drink down and stood to greet her.

Billy Graham followed close behind. He rushed to Cody's side and smiling a broad smile said, *"Mr. President, I would like to introduce Ms. Cody Rose of Orlando, Florida."*

This was a moment Cody would never forget, but not for the reasons you might think. No, it would remain frozen in Cody's memory because of what transpired next.

It hadn't happened in nearly a dozen years. Cody went down in a heap. The president and his religious advisor stood watching in disbelief as Cody lay on the floor convulsing uncontrollably. Her arms wailed wildly and her eyes rolled back in her head. *"What the hell happened"* Nixon bellowed? *"Jesus, Bill. Do something…"*

Cody's head hit the floor with such force her front teeth pierced her tongue. Blood was drooling from her mouth so badly Nixon got the dry heaves. The maître d rushed into the room to see what was causing all the commotion. When he saw Cody sprawled on the floor he stood alongside the other two men in disbelief. Finally the burly man guarding the door brushed past them. He picked the injured woman up and rushed out of the restaurant as other diners watched in horror.

The secret serviceman threw Cody into the backseat of the car that had pulled in behind the limo and climbed in after her. Another black suit climbed behind the wheel and the car peeled out. A few minutes later they carried Cody into the emergency room of Georgetown University Hospital.

Lesch-Nyhan had come rushing back with a vengeance. The illness never went away. It was always present, just in remission. The emergency room staff treated Cody with a strong dose of phenobarbital to countermeasure her symptoms. The drug worked quickly to diffuse the involuntary seizures and stop the biting, which now had progressed to her bottom lip. A portion of which was resting on Cody's chin.

Eight weeks later she was allowed to go home. Surgeons had reconstructed Cody's bottom lip and the wounds to her tongue had healed. Her pride was another matter. It was badly shaken. Cody was embarrassed beyond words. It had been years since she suffered an attack like that.

If her illness had not reared its ugly head that day Cody would have been dining with the President of the United States. While in the hospital she'd learned that at the moment of her arrival at the restaurant nearly half a million antiwar demonstrators had converged on the steps of the capitol to protest Nixon's escalation of the war.

When Cody pictured herself sitting in that fancy restaurant surrounded by fine china and museum quality artwork while these people marched just a few miles away she cringed. Why was the president not addressing those he was elected to lead? Why was he so damned adamant about having our nation's youth fight a war they could not hope to win? A war we had no justification fighting? Cody decided to step up to the plate.

Billy Graham was not home to take her call. The reverend was in California addressing a Christian businessmen's convention. The event was being held at the Cow Palace in San Francisco. Eleven hundred businessmen had paid a hundred dollars apiece to hear what the evangelist had to say.

Cody left Reverend Graham a message. After what happened at that fancy restaurant in Georgetown she wouldn't have been surprised if the preacher shunned her altogether. It must have been very embarrassing for him. After all the president was meeting with Cody at his bequest. What must Richard Nixon have thought?

Two days later Cody got a return phone call. Billy Graham was going to be in Florida at the end of the month and he wanted to get together. He seemed to know all about Cody's hospital stay in D.C. The reverend even knew the names of her surgeons and what they'd done to treat her.

They agreed to meet at his hotel. Graham was staying at the recently opened Grand Plaza on International Drive. Back then the evangelist was near the top of his popularity. Billy Graham had just recently addressed over a hundred thousand fervent young converts at the Cotton Bowl in Dallas, Texas. The youth had congregated there to find out what God had planned for their futures, convinced Graham was going to tell them. He was taking a few days off before moving on to his next project.

Cody had been instructed to approach the front desk and ask to be taken to Billy Sunday's room. She would then be escorted to Graham's suite. The reverend told her it was common for famous people like him to travel under assumed names.

Graham had borrowed the name from a turn of the century evangelist named William 'Sawdust' Sunday. Billy Sunday was a man the famous preacher likened himself to. He was a former professional baseball player who turned to Christ after attending a tent revival meeting in Chicago one summer day.

Billy Sunday is often referred to as the father of modern day evangelism. The preacher converted his flock by turning his tent meetings into a dramatic, antic filled vaudevillian production. He put on quite a show, taking quips from the popularity of vaudeville, the preeminent form of entertainment in those days.

At some point the bible thumping evangelist paired up with a talented trombone player named Homer Lee Rodeheaver. The bawdy musician and his bandmates would rev up 'Sawdust' Sunday's Holy Spirit filled audience with rollicking renditions of gospel tunes. That would set the stage for the prolific preacher to come out and shout fire and brimstone at his loving audience.

The two of them packed canvas sided tabernacles with souls for Christ on a nightly basis. Their revival meetings got so raucous Billy Sunday took to spreading sawdust on the ground inside his tent to muffle the noise of dancing boots. That's what earned him the nickname *Sawdust*.

In those days there was no such thing as speaking fees. Evangelist weren't paid salaries. They got what the crowd was willing to part with. Sawdust Sunday separated many a man from his paycheck. He figured the money was only going to be wasted on booze and ladies of the night anyway. Might as well be spent for the glory of the Almighty. Some would argue things haven't changed all that much.

Graham happened to be watching a ballgame on the television when Cody arrived. He turned the volume down and invited his guest to join him on the sofa. They talked about that day back at the restaurant. Cody had scared the bejesus out of Richard Nixon when she went down. He thought for sure she'd been shot. The president had become quite paranoid by then. He was always talking about some long haired hippie getting to close and taking him out.

Cody assured Billy Graham she was fine. She confessed she probably should have warned him about her condition, even though she hadn't had a spell like that in years. Cody told the evangelist she was trusting God to heal her of the affliction.

The reverend told Cody the reason he invited her to his room that day was because he was scheduled to have a conference call with the president. He was hoping she might be able to get through to him. Nixon was showing no sign of softening his stance on the war and his popularity was plummeting because of it.

Graham had been a hawk when it came to the Vietnam War but enough was enough. They had bombed the enemy into oblivion. So much so there was nothing left to blow up. The reverend hated to see his friend destroy his reputation for a cause he couldn't win. Nixon just would not listen.

No president wants to be the first commander in chief to lose a war, but those chink bastards just wouldn't quit. They dug themselves a network of intricate tunnels and moved around the Vietnamese countryside like a shipload of lice infested rodents. How the hell are you supposed to bomb that?

The phone rang right on queue. Reverend Graham rushed to answer it. He praised the president for the decisive action he'd taken against anti-war demonstrators, some of who'd marched on Arlington National Cemetery the previous day. Nixon had personally called the director of the cemetery to shut it down. Graham reminded the president that society cannot operate properly if subversion is allowed to flourish. *"God stands with those who stand for themselves,"* the famous evangelist declared.

Once Nixon had been sufficiently coddled the reverend told him there was someone there who wished to speak with him. He quickly handed the telephone receiver to Cody before the president had a chance to respond. Then Graham tapped the speaker button on the phone so he could listen in on the conversation. Cody gathered her wits then bravely spoke up.

"Good afternoon Mr. President," she said. *"I pray your day is going well?"* It wasn't. His wife was on one of her rampages again. They were becoming more and more frequent. The pressure was mounting to get the hell out of Vietnam and it was affecting her marriage. It had always been turbulent. Richard Nixon was a moody man and he could be difficult to live with.

The two of them had exchanged angry words moments before Nixon made his call. In fact he had booted his wife out of the oval office and slammed the door behind her. That was something the first lady truly despised. Now he was being forced to make nice with the sick friend of his spiritual advisor. It was bad timing.

"So how are you feeling these days Ms. Rose," the president unconvincingly asked? *"You gave us a scare. When I saw you drop down on the floor like that I was sure you'd been shot."*

Cody thanked the president for his concern and apologized for scaring him the way she did. She confessed she should have warned him about her condition. It had been in remission for so long she never saw it coming.

There was an uncomfortable silence on the other end of the line. It may have only lasted six or seven seconds but it seemed much longer. During that period of silence Cody had a flashback. She recalled the vision God had given her in a dream a little over a year before. In her dream she had been shown the image of a man who was suffering unfathomable pain.

The man had been given everything he needed to succeed at the highest level, and yet he had failed. He could have been a person of great honor, but he had dishonored himself. As a result of his failure the man in her dream was suffering terrible grief. It was the kind of grief that cannot be quelled or medicated away.

The cause of the man's pain came from without, not within. In that moment Cody realized who it was God had given her that word of knowledge for.

CODY ROSE
CHAPTER THIRTEEN

Proverbs 16:18. *"Pride goes before destruction, and a haughty spirit before the fall."*

Cody had received a word of knowledge from the Lord, but it wasn't meant for her. She was but a conduit. The word she'd been given was for the man she was speaking with on the telephone.

Richard Nixon had been elected by the people to lead this nation. He held the highest office in the land. Many would say the highest office in the world, but he'd veered off course. Rather than seek out the wisdom of the Lord the president was relying on his own intellect. He had allowed his pride to get in the way and he knew better.

The thirty-seventh President of the United States had been raised by devoutly religious parents. Throughout his childhood Nixon had attended an evangelical Quaker church. When it was time for college he went to an institution founded by Quakers. Richard Nixon knew the bible like the back of his hand. He also knew right from wrong. He just forgot.

Cody felt she'd wandered into unchartered territory. She was certain God had directed her steps. He had given her a mission, then put in place everything she would need to carry out that mission. All that was required of her was to be faithful to her calling. And so she spoke.

"Mr. President, I have something I need to tell you. I pray you won't be offended but I need to say it."

"What is it, Cody" Nixon responded? "Are you going to tell me I need to get the troops out of Vietnam? I'm hearing that from everyone these days. Believe me Ms. Rose, I'm not offended."

Okay. She had permission to continue. That was good. Now for the hard part. *"What I have to say to you is not from me,"* Cody explained. *"What I have to say is from God... I am just the messenger."*

Then she blurted it out. All ninety-four words. Live and in living color. *"Blessed is he who fears the Lord. For whomever hardens his heart will fall into calamity. The ruler who lacks understanding is a cruel oppressor, Mr. President. If a man turns his ear away from what the Lord is saying then even that man's prayers are an abomination unto Him. A ruler who conceals his transgressions will not prosper. It is not too late to fall on your knees and confess your sins, Mr. President. To be burdened with the blood of another is to be a fugitive until death... So sayeth the Lord."*

Cody's stark message was followed by an even longer silence than before. She glanced over at Billy Graham, who was leaning forward on the sofa with his mouth gaped open. A moment later President Nixon's voice reverberated out of the telephone speaker.

"Quoting from the book of Proverbs" he acknowledged. "Yes, I know it well, Ms. Rose. I used to study the Old Testament quite a bit when I was a youth. But that was long ago, Cody. People

change. Schoolboys grow up. We are dealing with the real world. A world full of problems that need solutions...and they need them fast."

"*I have been burdened with finding those solutions,*" the president continued. "*Do you understand that, Young Lady? I don't have time to wait for God to fix the world's problems. There are people out there that want to destroy us. I cannot let that happen. Not on my watch!*"

Nixon hadn't listened. That much was obvious. Cody wasn't preaching to him like some sidewalk vendor for Christ. She wasn't a pitchman trying to sell him a bill of goods he didn't want or need. She was delivering a message from God. A message meant for him and him alone. Richard Millhouse Nixon, the unequivocal leader of the free world.

The man was in denial. If perception is reality, and it is, then President Richard Nixon was living in a dark place. His perception of the world differed significantly from Cody's. Where she saw hope, he saw despair. Where she found comfort, he found sadness. What to her was unity, was to him dissolution.

Cody decided to meet him straight on. "*Mr. President, You need to stop whatever it is you think you need to do right now and find yourself a prayer closet. I have seen your pain. If you don't seek out God your burden will only increase. It will become more than you can bare. More than any man could possibly hope to bare.*"

She waited for a response. When none was forthcoming she continued. "*Humble yourself before the Lord, Mr. President. Ask*

Him for his guidance. You are a good man. You are an honest man. You are a child of the living God. So stop the killing. No more young men need die in a jungle ten thousand miles away from home. No more mothers have to bury their sons because of some insane war without end."

Cody could tell the president was still on the line. His breathing was heavy. At one point he muttered a few undecipherable words, mixed with a few she could make out. They weren't very nice. One time Cody heard him try to suppress a cough but it didn't work. Eventually he spoke.

"Bill, are you there? Cody, let me talk to Reverend Graham."

Cody handed the telephone receiver back to Billy Graham. He took it from her but didn't immediately raise it to his mouth. Instead the evangelist just looked at it, as though it were a big bar of lye soap.

When Billy Graham was a kid his mother would have to use a bar of lye soap on occasion. Those occasions being whenever a cuss word or a lie came out of his mouth. William and Morrow Graham were strict Calvinist. They raised their children to fear the Lord and follow the scriptures. William, Jr. was the oldest of the bunch. As such he was expected to be a role model for his younger siblings. Most of the time he was. Occasionally he wasn't.

His father was a dairy farmer. The Graham's owned a small spread in the hills overlooking Charlotte, North Carolina. They weren't wealthy folk, but they managed. William, Sr. taught his children to be self-sufficient and he taught them to follow God's law. Calvinist believe that God chooses man, not the other way around. In other words the Father selects those he deems as worthy of redemption and condemns the rest to eternal damnation. Hence the strict upbringing.

When Graham finally spoke into the receiver he told the president he hoped he would heed Cody's advice. President Nixon asked his spiritual advisor if he had put the young woman up to it. In fact he insisted that Graham had. Of course nothing could be further from the truth. Billy Graham had no idea what Cody was going to say. He'd only wanted her to try to convince the president to begin withdrawing some of the troops from Southeast Asia for his own good. He knew nothing of her dream.

She had tried. The thing about being a conduit for Christ is that you have to understand your role. You are not the Savior. It is not your responsibility to deliver souls. That choice is individual, and has to be made by the sinner. All one can do is present the truth to the best of their ability. God will handle it from there.

Cody had shared the Lord with hundreds of people since being saved. Maybe thousands? She'd never stopped to count them all. She had come to Florida to plant seed, and plant she did. What Cody was painfully aware of was the fact she had also been called to water that seed and to watch it grow. That meant being steadfast in her conviction and committed in prayer.

Nixon may have blown her off over the phone, but that wasn't the end of their conversation. Not as far as Cody was concerned. He was on her prayer list. Of course the sitting president always had been, but this time was different. Nixon was now on Cody's *priority* prayer list. That meant he had an intercessor who would continuously go before the Lord on his behalf. She would continuously hold the president up before the Lord's throne in faith. That lost sheep was now on her radar.

After Reverend Graham hung up the phone he dropped down on his knees and began to weep. Cody slid down beside the evangelist and took his hand in hers. Together they prayed for the President of the United States, asking God to open his eyes and ears to understand what the Lord would have him do. Then Graham did something totally unexpected. He looked Cody straight in the eye and said, *"Would you pray for me, Ms. Rose?"*

There it was again. Who in the world was she to pray for the most famous, most renowned evangelist in American history? This man had singlehandedly led untold millions to the Lord. He used every means of communication available to spread the message of God's love and redemption. Books, radio, television, crusades, all in the name of Jesus Christ...

Billy Graham had counseled every American president since Harry Truman. His services were broadcast by over twelve hundred radio stations across America. His divine message reached untold millions. Billy Graham was beloved throughout the world. If he had been catholic the pope probably would have made him a saint. Saint Billy. It had a certain ring to it.

Cody knew the answer to her question. Who was she? She was a child of the living God, that's who... Cody knew the Lord was no respecter of persons. He doesn't favor one child over another. Her prayers were as powerful as anyone's. As powerful as everyone's. She did as was requested...

CODY ROSE
CHAPTER FOURTEEN

Ted could only shake his head in amazement when he listened to Cody's stories. She was nearing the end of her life. A life cut short by an incurable illness. The psychotherapist wondered if there really was a God, and if so why he would allow his children to suffer so.

It wasn't the first time Ted had asked that question but this time it really did seem appropriate. The woman lying in that bed did not deserve to die. If he had his way Cody Rose would live forever. What the therapist failed to comprehend was that Cody would be doing just that regardless of what he believed.

Five years of college followed by another twenty-five as a professional therapist hadn't taught Ted what Cody was able to show him in less than a week. That for those who truly know God there is nothing to fear. The believer goes from glory to glory.

In other words they are transformed in His image. The believer mirrors the Lord they serve as they live the Christian life. They become glorified embodiments of Christ on the earth.

When Jesus died at Calvary He spent three days in the depths of hell atoning for our sin. When He arose Jesus left the tomb and appeared before his disciples. After reassuring them He had beaten death the Lord ascended into the clouds. He went from glory to glory. So shall we all who believe. Our bodies will remain here on earth for they are but a vessel, but we shall ascend with Him. That is the true wonderment of God's plan.

He who created us from the dust of the earth breathed life into us. Long after our human bodies return to the dust from whence they came the breath of God lives on. Let me explain it this way. We are not a person with a spirit living inside of us. We are a spirit living inside a person. When our human vessels have outlived their usefulness they wither away. Our spirit lives on. We ascend to Heaven just as the Lord before us. It is by that faith that we are saved.

It was Cody's prayer that Ted Grace learn this lesson. Not that her prayers were always answered. At least as far as she knew. Maybe John Calvin was right. Maybe God chooses who lives in eternity with him and who does not? She wasn't going to argue the semantics of theology. Cody just wanted people saved. It was her mission. She used the painting on her wall as an aid to help in her therapist's conversion.

During one of his longer visits Ted shared his story with Cody. Her therapist was born in upstate New York, the only child of a teenage mother. Ted's mom was only seventeen when she had him. Not that being a pregnant teenager was all that unusual. Lots of girls in the projects had babies while still in high school. A consequence of being poor. At least that's what Theodora Grace believed.

She'd dropped out of high school just before her junior year. Theodora always said one day she would go back and finish her education but she never did. She got a job cleaning offices for a law firm downtown. Shwartz, Selleck, and Zuckerman. The job didn't pay enough to cover the bills so she supplemented her income with occasional *'side work'*.

That's what Theodora called what she did on Saturday nights. *Side work.* Nowadays a girl in that profession is called a hooker. Theodora didn't do a lot of side work. One or two 'Johns' was usually enough to make up the difference between what she took home and what she paid out.

Her cleaning job down at the law office paid minimum wage. Theodora usually worked between twenty and thirty hours each week. It was up to her boss to determine how many. His name was Jimmy LaDuke.

LaDuke was a fifty-three year old former police officer. He'd been forced to resign from the police department after the way he treated a young lady he had stopped for a traffic infraction. The girl happened to be the daughter of a city court judge. After the young woman told her father what the officer did to her Jimmy was lucky to get off with just losing his job.

As the building maintenance foreman he supervised the cleaning operation. Eight women were responsible for cleaning two floors each. Theodora only had to worry about Shwartz, Selleck, and Zuckerman because the firm took up two entire floors.

Jimmy was the type of guy who thought he could do whatever he wanted to the hired help because he was the boss. It's amazing how just a tiny bit of authority can affect someone's behavior. The man was always making off color remarks to the cleaning ladies and trying to cop a quick feel.

What could they do about it? The owner of the building had given LaDuke the authority to bark out orders. Besides, he was a white man. All but one of the cleaning ladies was black. The white one was treated better than her counterparts. She got more hours too.

As for Theodora's so called *side work,* that was a story in itself. The teenage mother charged for her services on a sliding scale. The price depended on what the guys wanted. Oral was the cheapest. If you wanted more, well that cost more. If you were looking for something a bit kinkier the price went up accordingly.

Theodora set limits. She never did anything really out there. Not that she didn't get requests. That happened all the time. It never ceased to amaze her what some of those old white businessmen were into.

Ted's mother wasn't proud of how she spent her Saturday nights, but it wasn't as bad as some people made it sound. She was never beaten up or anything. Maybe that had more to do with luck than anything else. Theodora knew plenty of girls who were.

The worst encounter she ever had was more embarrassing than it was threatening. Theodora was standing in the shadow of a streetlamp a couple blocks away from the law offices she worked at when a car appeared out of nowhere. It came to a screeching halt right in front of her.

It was only nine o'clock in the evening but there was already a full moon. The big sphere seemed to be floating on a cloudless dark blue ocean. A moonbeam shown down on Theodora. Like a spotlight on a stage it seemed to follow her wherever she went.

The automobile sat there purring like a shiny metallic cat. A moment later the driver rolled down his window and asked Theodora if she was looking for a date. After all, she *was* wearing the uniform of her profession. Tight miniskirt, skimpy top, high heels, no panties, lots of makeup.

Theodora couldn't make out the face of the man behind the wheel. His identity was concealed by the darkness of the interior of the car. That didn't stop him from recognizing her though.

"Theodora..." the driver exclaimed! *"Is that you?"*

Theodora squinted in the direction of the voice and replied, *"Yes... Do I know you?"*

That's when she realized who it was. She was speaking to Sly Zuckerman, one of the law partners she worked for down at the firm. Theodora wanted to die. If she could have slithered down the storm drain that sat just beyond the lip of the curb she would have.

"Do you need a lift," Sly Zuckerman asked, as if the question somehow concealed his real reason for stopping. Theodora didn't know who was more embarrassed by their chance encounter. Him or her.

"Actually I do, Mr. Zuckerman" she lied. *"If it's not too much trouble. I live about a half mile south of here. I was walking home from the movie palace over on Main Street when I tripped on a crack in the sidewalk and broke the heel of my shoe."*

The excuse sounded authentic. Problem is they both knew it wasn't. Theodora didn't dress up like that to go to no movie palace. She was working the streets. The wealthy law partner felt a pang of guilt. He hollered out the window, *"Well, hop in."*

Ten minutes later Theodora was sitting on her sofa, penniless as the moment she left to work the streets. Her baby was fast asleep right where she'd left him less than an hour before. She picked the child up out of his bassinet and carried him to her bed. She needed to cuddle.

When Theodora got to work the following Monday evening Jimmy LaDuke gave her one of those *"I got the goods on you"* looks. He half smiled, half smirked an accusatorial comment. *"How was your weekend, Theodora?"*

LaDuke didn't wait for an answer. He jumped on the freight elevator and disappeared to another floor.

When Theodora got her paycheck the following Friday night it was for a much larger amount than normal. She had to look twice to be sure the check had her name on it. She'd been given a twenty-five percent pay raise.

She was pretty sure Zuckerman was the reason. He was trying to help her out. It was a nice jester but it wasn't going to change her lifestyle. Had the attorney not shown up last Saturday night Theodora would have likely earned considerably more than the raise she got, and she wouldn't have had to pay any taxes on it.

Theodora Grace never married, and she never had any more kids. She eventually got a better paying job. Theodora found work in a factory that made safety equipment for construction companies. The position allowed her to quit doing her so called 'side work'.

At that point in her life Theodora started going to church. She attended a predominantly black Pentecostal congregation located down the street from where she and her son lived. She found solace in the up tempo worship music and enjoyed the preaching of the head pastor. There were lots of other single mothers who went to church there too.

Ted was always somewhat quiet. As a child he spent a lot of his time studying other people. He had a yearning to understand what made people tick. When Ted turned twelve he got a job delivering the morning newspaper. He earned three dollars a week in tips. He's been working ever since.

The future therapist was a wiz in high school. Ted could have been anything he wanted to be, but for one undeniable thing. He was a young black man growing up in the 1950's. Any future for folks like him would certainly come with restrictions.

Upon graduating from high school Ted attempted to join the military. He could learn a marketable skill there. Maybe find a good job once he got out. Unfortunately he failed the medical procurement test. It seems Ted had an undescended testicle that had been that way since birth. You would have thought somebody would have noticed.

That debacle was followed by more bad news. Ted's mother got sick. Theodora contracted a lower respiratory illness that put her flat on her back. She was a tough gal but facing something as potentially dangerous as that was going to be quite demanding. Truth is she never did get better.

Theodora passed away a few months after Ted graduated from high school. The only good that came out of the situation was the fact that because of his mother's death Ted now qualified for a New York State educational scholarship intended for orphaned children. He chose to attend Buffalo State College.

Ted had a lot on his plate, what with his mother dying and all. When he finished his first year of college with a perfect 4.0 grade point average he surprised even himself.

The remainder of his collegiate education went much the same way. Ted excelled in his studies, while continuing to be a humble and thoughtful young man. He went about his business without much fanfare. While most of his fellow students were attending weekend frat parties and other such shenanigans Ted stayed in his room and studied for his future.

✝

CODY ROSE
CHAPTER FIFTEEN

Ted went on to earn his master's degree in mental health counseling. He graduated from Stetson University, a small school in Deland, Florida. After spending four years freezing his ass off in Buffalo, New York he was more than ready to enjoy some warmer weather. Florida fit the bill like a warm pair of fleece lined pajamas.

In order to get his state certification Ted was required to work under the auspices of a licensed mental health counselor. Saint Raphael's Hospital afforded him that opportunity. He went to work for the hospital immediately following his graduation from Stetson.

His department head was also a Stetson grad. Mark Williams happened to be an avid basketball fan. He never missed a home game at his alma mater. Hadn't since he was a student there over twenty years ago. Williams managed to talk Ted into going to a few games with him.

Prior to taking the position at St Raphael's Ted hadn't really been interested in sports. The intercollegiate athletic program at Stetson University was small time comparatively speaking, but it was growing in stature. They weren't exactly Florida State yet, but The Stetson University Hatters were competitive.

For the first six months Ted was working at Saint Raphael's he and his boss spent as much time talking college basketball as they did mental health counseling. These days Ted still takes in an occasional Hatter's game, but he is much more inclined to watch sports on TV.

Mark Williams retired a few years after Ted arrived on the scene. Ted took over the palliative care department from him. The position provided him an opportunity to develop his own intervention program. Saint Raphael's had always concentrated its counseling efforts on patients recovering from traumatic injuries. Folks who arrived in the emergency room with severed limbs or broken necks. The needs of the dying were handed off to hospice workers.

Hospice has its place in palliative care medicine. They help to ensure a terminal patient receives enough pain medication to give them peace of mind, and enough companionship to allay any fears of abandonment.

Ted's intervention program was different. He addressed the needs of the soon to be departed in a practical sense, often utilizing professionally trained end of life doulas to accomplish that goal.

Doulas were originally used to provide emotional support for women in the latter stages of pregnancy. Their main function was to promote a safe environment and establish confidence in a prenatal woman. A time when many first time mothers feel quite vulnerable.

End of life doulas provide a similar service. They prepare terminally ill patients for their journey by tailoring the care they receive to their particular situation. Each patient is unique and their needs reflect that.

As a psychotherapist Ted knew most terminal patients suffer terrible anxiety over things they can no longer control. By utilizing end of life doulas the therapist is able to provide his patients with some sense that they haven't completely relinquished authority over their own lives.

There are no references to God in Ted's program. Therapy is limited to the practical needs of the patient. Things like their financial concerns and legal questions that may not have been answered? What will happen to their body when they die? Do they have a say in what funeral arrangements have been made? Does anybody care that they are dying?

Of course a patient's physical comfort is part of the equation too. Part of Ted's job is to make sure any symptoms associated with a terminally ill patient's particular area of concern are immediately addressed. He coordinates with other health care professionals to ensure the patient's journey is as painless and worry free as possible.

Ted Grace's palliative approach to treating terminal patients had never been tried before. Prior to his intervention program hospitals treated a dying patient's level of pain, using sedatives and other medications to limit their discomfort. The emotional condition of the terminal patient was for the most part ignored. I mean what could be done. They were going to die.

Ted aimed to treat the psychological aspects of dying. He wanted his patients to approach the reality of death in a positive light. He encouraged them to reflect on a life lived rather than a life ending. Death was an unavoidable condition of being born. Why not approach it with a sense of wonderment?

The therapist didn't like interjecting religion into the equation. Everyone had their own interpretation of what that inferred. He knew the fear of going to hell was rampant in patients who dwelled on the perceived mistakes they'd made in their lives.

Ted likened death to being born. It wasn't necessarily an end, but a new beginning. I know that sounds like religion but it's not. Let me explain.

Religion has conditions. You live a good wholesome existence and you are rewarded in the afterlife. You confess your sins and you are forgiven. You accept your infallible nature and seek out a supernatural being who will save you from eternal damnation.

Ted's response to all that spiritual mumbo jumbo was phooey. He wanted his terminal patients to question the possibility their journey wasn't ending at all. It was altogether possible life was just entering a new phase, God or no God. Who could say for certain what happens when we die?

Consider the moment a life is born. A fetus is being forcefully extracted from an environment it has come to rely on for its very existence. It is being ripped away from its only known source of nourishment and oxygen supply. What once was a warm, safe, and hospitable habitat is now rejecting it without recourse. Is that not like dying?

On the other hand Ted didn't ignore the fact that life may indeed just stop being. He didn't try to get his patients to buy in to his notion that there could be more. If life did end than it was important people not fear the inevitable. Besides tending to his patient's immediate needs and concerns Ted's job was to bring comfort and understanding to a subject no one ever wants to have to deal with.

"Acceptance is the better part of valor." Ted used the self-altered idiom to explain why fear was the enemy to those facing death. One could always hope. Miracles happened. A person's ultimate fate wasn't necessarily written in stone, but there comes a time when we all have to accept our own mortality. It is a part of life.

Ted Grace would continue to implement the intervention program he developed at St Raphael's until the day someone showed up and turned his world upside down. It wasn't what he learned about Cody Rose's life that upset the therapist's proverbial applecart. It was her death. More specifically it is what Ted experienced after learning of her death.

✝

CODY ROSE
CHAPTER SIXTEEN

The Community Housing Fund's first rehabilitation project was a huge three story structure located on South Pine Avenue in downtown Orlando. When it was first built the brick building was home to a wagon wheel manufacturing plant. It suffered a long period of decline after the plant closed its doors, a victim of the Great Depression.

The building sat idle for nearly two decades. Eventually an investor purchased the property and converted the interior into office space. He then sold the building to an Orlando law firm. Garret Price & Associates.

Attorney Garret Price had been active in local politics. He served two terms as an Orlando City Councilman before running for a seat in the Florida State Legislature. He held that post for ten years. Price eventually lost his legislative seat to a republican neophyte with deep pockets.

It was a bitter pill to swallow. Price's defeat gave republicans control of the Florida State Legislature. The first thing they did was pass legislation allowing them to realign Florida's legislative districts. In essence they gave themselves a strategic advantage.

Upon returning to his law firm Garret Price dedicated himself to fighting the practice of gerrymandering. His efforts paid off for a while. The courts put strict limitations on the practice. Unfortunately those efforts have since been overturned.

Before he died Garret gifted the South Pine Street property to the city of Orlando. City officials then leased the building to the Community Housing Fund.

The nonprofit converted the building into dwellings to house the poor and disenfranchised. Many of the buildings tenants were previously homeless. Some were recovering drug addicts, others recently released ex-convicts reentering society. There were even a few down on their luck Vietnam War vets who'd come home to find their lives turned upside down.

Cody's job with CHF required her to live on site. She was provided with an apartment in the South Pine Street property. It wasn't glamourous, but it was comfortable. She furnished it with eclectic pieces salvaged from area consignment stores.

As you entered the building you found yourself standing in a large brick faced foyer facing a six foot wide mahogany staircase. Just to the left of the staircase was a long hallway. The first door you came to was Cody's apartment. It was identified with a brightly painted sign on the door that read, WELCOME TO THE OFFICE OF CHF ADMINISTRATOR CODY ROSE.

That sign is how the emergency medical responders located her when they arrived at the site. A faded logo barely visible on the front of the building told them they were in the right place. It depicted a muleskinner, whip in hand, leading a team of mules.

The person making the call to 911 hadn't been very specific on the address. He just said it was the old wagon wheel factory on South Pine Street. He told the operator to have the driver look for the building with the muleskinner painted on it.

The man was a Vietnam vet. He lived on the second floor directly above Cody's apartment. He had gone down to ask if he could borrow her iron because he had an appointment at the VA in the morning and his shirt was wrinkly. He was standing in Cody's office hollering into the telephone, *"HELP... HELP... IT's MISS ROSE. I think she's hurt..."*

When the EMT's rushed in Cody was lying on the floor in a fetal position. She was bleeding profusely from a nasty gash on her forehead. The technician treating her assumed she must have struck her head on the hard wooden floor when she fell.

Truth is Cody had smashed her head against the floor multiple times while waiting for help to arrive. It was an uncontrollable reflex caused by her Lesch-Nyhan. Her blood soaked face was bloated and contorted in a horrific grimace.

What no one knew at the time was that Cody's kidneys were failing. There were signs. Her face was badly swollen, especially around the eyes. So were her ankles. She had been itching too. Cody had scratched herself raw all around her belly button. She'd actually scraped gouges into her skin. Unfortunately her injuries were hidden by her clothing. The medical responders completely missed it.

As the first responders lifted her into the ambulance Cody looked at the poor fellow who had stumbled upon her convulsing body. She mouthed a few words but the guy couldn't make them out. Cody was trying to tell the soldier, *"God bless you. You are my hero."*

When they got to the emergency room Cody was examined by a team of doctors. She wasn't yet able to talk so she couldn't explain her illness. It took multiple lab tests and a thorough examination by an experienced neurologist to determine the cause of Cody's attack

The neurologist had been in practice for over fourteen years and this was the first female case of Lesch-Nyhan Syndrome he had ever seen. He knew Cody's prognosis wasn't good. He knew she would most likely never leave that hospital alive. All they could hope to do was try to make the time she had remaining as comfortable as possible.

Cody would be assigned to Ted Grace and his caring staff. The psychotherapist had developed an award winning palliative care program. Cody would be sedated for the night and if she was still alive in the morning she would be put on his schedule.

✝

CODY ROSE
CHAPTER SEVENTEEN

Which brings us back to where we began. The story has been told. Cody was not going to be leaving Saint Raphael's Hospital alive. She knew it and her therapist knew it. So why would Ted Grace go to so much trouble?

His motivation came from wanting to make everything better. The psychotherapist spent most of his time trying to compensate for the fact he couldn't. He and Cody spent their last few hours together rehashing all they'd discussed leading up to that point. Ted felt like he knew Cody pretty well. She'd certainly lived an interesting life. He knew of no one else who even came close.

Cody knew Ted pretty well too. Her therapist was a smart guy. He'd done okay for himself, especially when you consider the disadvantages he'd had to overcome. Cody wanted more than anything for Ted to accept Jesus Christ as his lord and savior. She did not want to go to her grave thinking she hadn't done everything humanly possible to make that happen.

Unfortunately it didn't. At least not then. The truth is Cody did do everything humanly possible to get Ted saved. But in the end it was his decision, like it is for all of us.

There is an idiom that says you can lead a horse to water but you can't make him drink. Well Ted was offered the cup of redemption. He just refused to put it to his lips.

Still the seed had been planted. Remember the flower that sprang from the ground at Cody's feet back in New Mexico? If

God could make something as beautiful as that grow out of the hard dry desert soil then he could work a miracle in Ted's life.

The next morning the therapist began his rounds right on time. Ted had seven patients on his schedule. Cody was his first, as had been his pattern. No sooner did he step off the elevator when an orderly came rushing around the corner pushing a stretcher. A young nurse was accompanying him. She held the elevator door open as the orderly and the stretcher disappeared inside.

Ted had noticed the stainless steel bars of the stretcher were in the up position. That told him the bed was occupied. It wasn't an unusual sight, especially in the morning. Most medical procedures are scheduled for that time of day. He continued on his rounds without giving it another thought.

When he got to Cody's room Ted paused in the hallway to review her chart, which was hanging on a hook near the door. He noticed the overnight nurse had not entered any remarks. Not a single word about her vital signs or bowel movements. No mention of what she'd eaten for breakfast. That gave him reason to ponder.

He peered back down the hall, trying to recall if he'd seen the face of the patient who was on that stretcher being pushed into the elevator. Ted could tell you in detail what the orderly looked like. He could tell you that the nurse was young and quite attractive. What he couldn't recall was actually seeing the patient. He knew the stretcher was occupied. The side rails were in the up position.

Ted's movements became measured as he entered Cody's room. As if he knew what he was going to find before taking his first step.

Cody was not there. Her bed had been stripped of its bedding. It sat in a pile at the foot of the bed. The room felt as sterile as a test tube. Ted sat on the edge of the bed and revisited some of the conversations he and his patient had shared that week. A thought brought a smile to his face. *"Just who had been therapizing who?"*

The therapist made his way to the nurse's station. The charge nurse was sitting behind her desk busily updating patient's records and took no notice of him. When Ted cleared his throat to get her attention she stood and offered an apology. *"Sorry. We lost two patients overnight. I'm playing catch up."*

"No need to explain," Ted responded. *"I just wanted to inquire about one of my patients. I have a therapy session scheduled with Ms. Rose this morning."*

The charge nurse was well aware of the unique relationship the therapist had with this particular patient. Everyone on the floor knew. She had to tell him Cody was one of the patients who'd died during the night. *"Ms. Rose went quietly,"* she offered. *"She passed without incident. One of my student nurses just assisted an orderly taking her down to the morgue."*

A tear formed in the corner of Ted's eye. He wiped it away before it had a chance to drop, then thanked the nurse and headed back down the hallway. When he got to Cody's room he stood in the doorway for a moment before entering.

The room had a different smell to it. A clean smell, like it had been scrubbed with bleach. There was a fresh set of sheets sitting in a corner chair waiting for someone to come along and put them in their place. Ted walked in and turned his gaze toward the painting on Cody's wall. The one she had been so enamored with.

He had an inclination to confiscate it. Ted wanted to take the painting as a memento of their friendship. Hell, the hospital wouldn't miss it. He would buy the damn thing from them if he had to.

But he couldn't. The painting was gone. Ted stood staring at a blank wall, and it was staring back at him. He bolted out of the room and made his way back to the nurse's station. When he got there he took a moment to gather his composure then asked, "Nurse... What the hell happened to the painting in Cody's room?"

"Painting," the nurse responded? "What painting?"

The therapist was beside himself. He insisted the charge nurse accompany him back to the room, which she did. When they got there nothing had changed. The wall facing Cody's bed was as bare as a chimpanzee's feet. There were no paintings hanging on any walls in that room. Saint Raphael's didn't put artwork on the walls in patient's rooms.

"The only place the hospital hangs artwork is in the front lobby," the nurse insisted. "That's it. No place else. The only thing hanging on a patient's wall is a television set."

Ted would have none of it. *"Hogwash..."* he bellowed. *" I saw that painting with my own two eyes. You couldn't miss it. The damn thing took up half the wall. Somebody took that painting down."*

The therapist walked over and touched the spot where it had been hanging. Then he turned and gave a full length description of the piece.

"It was of a door. A really thick wooden door. The door was encased in an old stone wall. Ms. Rose pointed out the variance of colors in the lines of the wood. The ambers and the cinnamons. I hadn't seen them until she pointed them out."

The nurse stood speechless. She had been assigned to that floor for nearly ten years. She'd been in that hospital room a thousand times. There was no painting hanging on that wall. Never had been.

Ted went on with his diatribe anyway. He was certain the painting had been there. *"The door didn't have a knob,"* he insisted. *"I asked Cody about that. She told me there was no knob because you couldn't just open the door and enter through it. You had to be invited in."*

The therapist took a deep breath. He was exasperated and his voice reflected it. It became higher pitched as the exasperation level increased. *"There were two chubby pink angels hovering just above the doorway, Nurse. One on either side. Cody called them cherubim, and she said angels are actually quite strong."*

Ted could tell the charge nurse thought he was crazy. It was written all over her face. "GODDAMN IT," he argued, "*I KNOW WHAT I SAW...*"

The look on the nurse's face changed to one of compassion. She walked over and patted Ted on the shoulder. It was not done in a condescending way. She understood what was happening. The man had broken the golden rule of medicine. *'Do not allow yourself to get emotionally attached to a patient.'*

It was considered a big no-no for those who worked in this particular field. If a medical professional were to do that with every patient they wouldn't be able to carry out the duties of their position. The nurse didn't say anything more. She didn't have to. She just turned and walked out of the room.

✝

CODY ROSE
CHAPTER EIGHTEEN

So it had come to this. Just like that Cody was gone. Ted never got to say goodbye. The therapist didn't bother to hold it back this time. He let the tears come. They welled up in his eyes and rolled down his cheeks like raindrops from heaven.

It felt good to cry. In the midst of his sorrow Ted actually laughed about his predicament. Here he was a grown man. A trained psychotherapist with many years of experience allowing himself to be swept away by the passing of a patient.

The woman had Lesch-Nyhan Syndrome for God's sake. No one survives that. The illness is a killer, and a cruel one at that. Ted knew his patient had done well to live as long as she did. He stared long and hard at the blank wall at the foot of the bed. What had he seen? Was it all in his head? Had he dreamt it? Did Cody Rose even exist?

As he started for the door Ted was in a confused stupor. The therapist knew that sometimes things happen that simply defy explanation. Anomalies do exist. Curiosities no one can account for in any cohesive way. Perhaps this had been one of those times.

Before he walked out of the room Ted turned to take one last look. At the empty bed. At the blank wall at the foot of it. At his own life. He hoped it would be a very long time before he had to come back here. If he had his way no future patients would be assigned to this room. This was Cody's room.

That's when something caught his eye. It appeared to be some type of card or envelope. It was lying under the bed, far enough in you could only see it from a distance. Ted walked back over and stooped down to take a better look. It appeared to be a photograph. The therapist got down on his hands and knees to retrieve it. It would be some time before he stood back up.

With his hands shaking Ted reached under the bed and slid the photograph towards him. When he picked it up he saw it was actually a 3 X 5 inch postcard. On one side was a picture of a thick wooden door encased in an old gray stone wall, two chubby pink cherubim floating on either side.

Ted's emotions overtook him. He knew what he had to do. Hell he was already on his knees anyway. The therapist held the post card tight to his chest and with his voice trembling asked God to forgive him of his sins.

He thanked the Lord for sending his Son Jesus Christ to take on the sins of the world so that he might be saved. He asked God to come into his heart and forever change him. After praying the sinner's prayer Ted flipped the postcard over. There on the other side Cody had written these words:

"Ted, I want to thank you for everything you did for me. You are a true friend. The day I met you my destiny became clear. I believe the Lord brought us together. He knew I would tell you of His divine glory, and that you would listen. It is important that you know the truth of Jesus Christ. That Jesus is the only begotten Son of God. He is the resurrection and the life, and all who believe in Him shall live with Him in eternity. We as joint heirs with Christ

will inherit the kingdom of God. *So I invite you to come. Knock at the door of eternal life. I promise you will be welcomed in.*

The card was signed... *Cody Rose.*

†

THE END

ABOUT THE AUTHOR:

Frederick C. Henderson was born in Montreal, Canada. His family immigrated to the United States when he was just a small child, settling in upstate New York. After his retirement from the U.S. Postal Service Frederick moved to the Daytona Beach area and began writing his first novel, EARLY RETIREMENT (Murder in Daytona) which was published in May, 2013.

EARLY RETIREMENT has been called a riveting murder mystery. The novel was selected as a *'Book of the Month'* selection by the Daytona Beach News Journal. A critique written by the Ithaca Press proclaims *"EARLY RETIREMENT is a compelling story with an immensely interesting cast of characters. It grabs the reader with such intense shocking images they can't help but continue reading."* The critique goes on to suggest the author has proven himself an outstanding storyteller.

Frederick hopes his readers will enjoy 'CODY ROSE' as much as they did his initial offering. Though it is a totally different genre the storytelling is just as enthralling and the characters just as engaging.

PEACE!

Made in United States
Orlando, FL
30 August 2024